Once Upon a Marigold

Once Upon a Marigold

JEAN FERRIS

SCHOLASTIC INC.

New York Toronto London Auckland Sydney
Mexico City New Delhi Hong Kong Buenos Aires

ISBN 0-439-57624-5

Copyright © 2002 by Jean Ferris. All rights reserved.
Published by Scholastic Inc., 557 Broadway, New York, NY 10012,
by arrangement with Harcourt, Inc. SCHOLASTIC and associated logos
are trademarks and/or registered trademarks of Scholastic Inc.

12 11 10 9 8 7 6 5   4 5 6 7 8/0

Printed in the U.S.A.   40

First Scholastic printing, October 2003

Text is set in Berling

Designed by Lydia D'moch

For A. G. F., my prince charming

Part One

1

Edric knew he should head for home. It would be dark soon, and even though he was as familiar with his part of the forest as he was with the back *and* the front of his hand, there were dangers when the lights went out—wild animals, evil spirits, big glowing eyes attached to who-knew-what, stuff like that. But Beelzebub and Hecate were having such a good time sniffing under every bush and barking all the grouse out from their hiding places that Ed was reluctant to spoil their fun. Besides, he'd been having a very good day of gathering.

Some days there was nothing; nobody passing through the forest dropped a thing. But today he'd found a ring with a big shiny pink stone, a collapsible telescope, a book of Greek myths, an almost-new leather jerkin, and a flask half full (he knew there were some people who would have said half empty) of a quite palatable wine—rather frisky, with some floral notes and a nice, lingering, jaunty sort of finish. It had been a very good day indeed.

He heard the dogs yapping their heads off up ahead. Not an encouraging sign. He could tell Bub was working himself into a state, trying to act as fierce as he looked, and Cate was overemoting, as usual. Whatever they were barking at must have gone straight up a tree, taken off for parts unknown, or had a coronary.

"Hey, you guys!" Ed yelled. "Cut that out!" He came through the trees and saw the two dogs—big shaggy Beelzebub and petite well-groomed Hecate—in front of a clump of bushes, carrying on as if they didn't have a brain in either of their heads.

"Hey!" he yelled again. "Stop that!"

Abruptly they stopped barking. But both noses were pointed at the bushes, both tails out straight and quivering.

"What's in there?" Ed asked nervously. The light was fading through the trees, casting long shadows that wavered and fooled the eye into thinking threatening things lurked in the gloom. Or maybe the shadows weren't fooling at all.

"Come on," Edric said in a low voice. "Let's go home."

The dogs didn't move.

"Would you listen to me?" he pleaded, peering anxiously around as the light grew dimmer. If only he'd thought to bring along some squirrel knuckles, their favorite treat, he could have lured them away easily.

He wasn't supposed to be snaring squirrels, of course, since these were King Swithbert's woods, or maybe King Beaufort's—it was hard to tell where the boundaries between the two kingdoms lay—but who was going to miss a few squirrels when there were so many? Well, the other squirrels, maybe, but he didn't let himself think about that. Hayes Centaur, King Swithbert's gamekeeper, was conscientious (unlike King Beaufort's more laid-back Claypool Sasquatch) and would love nothing better than to catch Edric poaching a squirrel, but even *he* couldn't keep count of all the squirrels, or tell which were Swithbert's and which were Beaufort's.

Ed pushed his way between the dogs, who were quivering so hard that they sent up a faint hum. He extended the collapsible telescope and poked it gingerly into the bushes. "Hello?" he said tentatively.

"Hello," came a small voice.

Edric and the dogs jumped in unison.

"Who's in there?" Ed demanded gruffly, hoping he sounded seven feet tall instead of his actual three feet, four inches.

"Me," came the small voice. And a handsome little boy with big brown eyes and tousled brown hair—a few leaves clinging haphazardly to it—stuck his head out of the bushes. "Will those dogs eat me?" he asked solemnly.

Edric was so relieved, his knees went weak. "Naw," he said. "This one"—he put his hand on Beelzebub's shaggy neck and felt the dog's shivers of terror—"is a coward who hides behind his big bark. And this one"—he scratched Hecate's ears—"is a show-off who just wants to be the center of attention." Cate wagged her plumy tail vigorously and grinned.

"Who are *you*?" the boy asked, crawling farther out of the bushes.

"Edric's my name. But mostly I'm called Ed. And who are *you*?"

"Christian," the boy said. "I'm six."

"Well, come out of there, Christian, and tell me what you're doing here."

Christian crawled all the way out from the bushes and stood up. "I'm almost as big as you," he said, surprised.

Ed pulled himself to his full height. "I'm tall for a troll," he said defensively.

"I've never met a troll before," Christian said.

Ed stuck out his hand and shook Christian's. "Now you have. And what about you?"

"I'm a boy," Christian said seriously. "Can't you tell?"

"Well, sure. I know you're a boy. What I want to know is, where are your folks? It's almost dark out here."

"I don't know where they are now. They looked for me for a long time, but their voices got farther and farther away until I couldn't hear them at all."

"You mean you were hiding from them?" Ed asked. "Why?"

"I don't want to live with them anymore. It's too hard."

"So you thought you'd live in the *forest*? Do you have any idea how hard *that* would be for somebody wearing a . . . a . . . What is that? A velvet suit?"

"What should I wear instead?"

"What I mean is, somebody like you doesn't know anything about living in a forest. That cup of tea is definitely not down your alley, if you know what I mean. What would you do for shelter? Food? Heat? Protection?"

"I was going to live in that bush." Christian gestured. "It has berries on it."

Ed rolled his eyes. "I can see I'm beating my head against a dead horse. There are berries now because it's summer. There won't be any in a few more weeks." He considered for about half a second and then said, "You'd better come home with me. I can take you back to your folks in the morning."

Christian's lower lip came out. "I'll go with you now, but I won't go home in the morning. I don't even know where home is."

Ed put his hand on Christian's shoulder. "Let's get out of here. It'll be pitch-dark in a few minutes, and I don't want to run into any more surprises. We can finish this conversation once we're inside. Come on, Bub. Get going, Cate. Let's get this show on the ball."

Cate scampered ahead, throwing herself into her performance as a courageous guide dog. Bub, sticking close to Ed, could feel a sick headache coming on—he always got one after he'd had to be brave—and he could hardly wait to flop down in front of the fire and pull himself together.

"What's that shiny blue stuff up there?" Christian asked after they'd wound along narrow rutted paths for a while, doing their bests not to run into any trees, fall in any streams, or become supper for anything else wandering around out there.

"Where?" Ed asked. "Oh, yeah. Great! That's the cave. We're almost home." The dogs ran ahead and disappeared into the shadows.

"You live in a cave?" Christian asked. "Why is it blue?"

"It's blue, and red, and green, and pink, and purple, and yellow, too," Ed said. "It's a big cave with lots of rooms, and in each room the walls and ceilings are studded with a different kind of crystal. I don't know how, but they glow in the dark. Kind of pretty, don't you think?"

"Yeah," Christian breathed as they approached. "It looks like magic."

"Well, maybe it is. I don't know of another cave like it. When I discovered it, the entrance was all blocked by rocks and dirt. I was sick of being a nomad and knew I'd finally found my home. Trolls have to spend at least one hundred years of their lives in a cave; did you know that? It's a tradition. I've been here, oh, must be one hundred and seventeen years now."

In the large yellow-crystal room that Ed used for his main parlor, he built up the fire, stumbling repeatedly over Bub, who was laid out in front of it like a hearth rug, breathing deeply in relief at being safe at home.

For supper there was leftover raccoon ragout, seasoned with wild garlic, onion, parsley, sage, rosemary, and thyme. There were acorn-meal biscuits and new strawberries and the wine Ed had found that day. When it was all gone, Ed let out a satisfied burp.

Christian imitated him and giggled. "If I did that at home, I'd be sent to my room," he said. "Actually, I'd be dragged off to my room, probably by my ear."

A bit drastic for a burp, Ed thought, but maybe he'd lived in a cave for so long he'd lost whatever social graces he might once have had.

"And you can forget about taking me back there," Christian went on. "I'm tired of being told what to do, and of being too clean, and of not being able to make a mess. Inventing is messy, and that's what I like to do. My parents will be glad I'm gone."

"I thought they searched for you all afternoon."

"Oh, they'll forget about me pretty soon. They have lots of other kids," Christian said. "Father never listens to me. And Mother only cares about how clean I am—and I'm never clean enough. The rest of the time she just wants to play bezique and piquet with her lady friends."

Ed could see there was no point in arguing with this kid. He figured he could manage to put up with the little squirt for one night and then he'd track down the parents and hand him over. "Come on," he said. "It's late. You can wear this for a nightshirt." He handed the boy a shirt of thin cambric that he had found beside a pond. Well, he had to admit he could see the owner of the shirt splashing in the pond, but he'd left him his boots and his breeches, hadn't he? What else did a body need to get home in on a warm summer day?

Ed made a bed for Christian out of furs in the dark-blue-crystal room. Sleeping in there was like sleeping up in the night sky with the glitter of stardust all around you. The little boy looked quite happy bedded down in the furs, the sleeves of his nightshirt rolled up four and a half times. As soon as he put his head down, both dogs came padding in to flop on either side of him.

With an arm around each furry neck, he murmured sleepily, "You can throw that stupid velvet suit away. I'm never wearing it again." Then his eyes closed, and three sets of soft snores rose to the shining ceiling.

"Who does he think he is?" Ed muttered, picking up the trail of discarded clothing as he went back to the fire in the yellow-crystal room. "Imperious little son of a gun, acting like some big cheese in a small pond, expecting me to pick up after him like I was his servant."

He dropped the clothing in front of the fire and sat on the picnic rug he'd found years before, way over on King Beaufort's side of the forest. It was a picnic that had been interrupted suddenly; he could tell that much from the scattered plates and utensils and food. Not that there was much food left. Whatever animal had come upon the picnickers had enjoyed the meal more than they had. But Ed had enjoyed the kitchenware, the hamper, the big napkins embroidered with the letter *B*, and the rug, all of which he'd hauled home.

He shook out each small item of clothing and dusted it off. As he folded the velvet shorts, he heard a faint tinkle. In the pocket he found a gold chain with a golden charm hanging from it. The charm was in the shape of a bird unlike any Ed had ever seen in the forest, though that certainly didn't mean it didn't exist. The world was full of fantastical creatures. The bird seemed to be part pheasant and part eagle.

Ed returned the chain to the pocket. Under other circumstances he would have added it to his collection, but he had a feeling the kid's parents would notice if it was missing. Then he wrapped the stack of clothing in one of the big picnic napkins, stashed the bundle in the hamper, and settled down with his briar pipe and the book of Greek myths. Nothing like a little fratricide, patricide, matricide, and infanticide to send a fellow right off to sleep.

2

In the morning Christian folded his arms across his sturdy chest and said, "I'm not going out there with you. I told you I didn't want to be found."

"Oh, give me a break," Ed said, annoyed. The last thing he needed was a little boy, for pete's sake. "What can be so bad about going home?"

"I told you. There're too many stupid rules. You can't talk unless somebody asks you a question, even if you have something really good to say, and you can't hit your brother even if he's done something mean, and you have to have all those boring lessons, and—"

"But those are normal rules parents are supposed

to have," Ed interrupted. "Mine did, and I..." He almost said, "...and I never ran away." But he had. Every one of his eight brothers had, too. It was a troll tradition. "Well, anyway, if I let you stay here, I'd feel like a kidnapper or something."

Christian stuck out his lower lip and said, "If you tell anybody where I am, I'll tell them you *did* kidnap me. And that you were going to ask for a whole lot of money to give me back, and that even after you got the money, you were still going to torture me and then kill me. How do you think my parents would like that?"

Beads of sweat popped out on Ed's forehead. Why, the kid was a scoundrel. A con man. A rascal and a rogue. And there wasn't a thing Ed could do about it. He *did* know what those parents would think. And what they would probably do to him. Who would believe the truth coming from him, a mere forest troll, compared to a big lie coming from an adorable kid with the heart of a weasel?

"Jeez," he said. "You're a menace."

"Only when I have to be," Christian said with an unhappy little tremble in his voice, and went to lie in front of the fire with Cate and Bub.

And as much as Ed wanted to turn him over his

knee and give him a good spanking, he couldn't help noticing how relieved the boy looked to be piled up with the undemanding, comforting dogs.

Christian stayed there almost all day, dozing or playing with the dogs, not asking for anything, just saying "Thank you" very politely when Ed brought him something to eat.

"I've got to go out for a while," Ed said. At Christian's ferocious look, he added, "And I'm not telling anybody anything, so quit giving me that black eye."

Outside, the forest was unusually still, as if all the creatures in it, even the fiercest, ugliest, most fire-breathing ones, were holding their breaths. Even the leaves hung motionless in the dusty golden sunlight. Ed stood still himself and listened. Far off he heard the yodel of hunting horns and the baying of bloodhounds, and he understood why the forest creatures were lying low. Nobody likes to be hunted down.

But maybe the horns and the dogs weren't hunting animals. Maybe they were after a little boy. Ed set out through the trees, following the sounds—but they just kept getting farther and farther away. And with them went his chance to unload the little rapscallion.

What had possessed him to bring the kid home with him? If he'd left him in the bushes, his parents would doubtless have found him by now. As the sounds finally faded completely away and darkness began to settle around him, Ed sighed and turned toward home. Oh well. He'd buttered his bread, and now he had to lie in it.

CHRISTIAN WAS WAITING by the fire, one arm clutched tightly around each dog, his eyes wide.

Ed flung his jacket onto a chair. "They were out there, looking for you, but they're gone now."

The dogs went tearing out of the cave. They'd felt some instinctive protectiveness toward the boy and wouldn't have left him alone. But now that Ed was home, they were way overdue for a run.

"Will they come back?" Christian asked.

"The dogs? Of course. They live here."

"Not them. The people looking."

"How should I know? How bad do they want you?"

"Maybe not very much. They don't like my ideas."

"Ideas? What kind of ideas can a little kid have?" Ed asked. "For pete's sake."

"I have ideas," Christian said indignantly, coming over to Ed, tripping on the dirty tail of the big cambric shirt he still wore.

"Tell me one," Ed said. He needed some ideas himself. Like, what the heck was he going to do with a kid?

"I think people shouldn't have children unless they really want them," Christian said.

Well, Ed agreed with that idea. He definitely didn't want a kid. "What else?" Ed asked grumpily.

"I think people should be nice to each other and share what they have with people who need things."

Ed swallowed hard. He couldn't exactly disagree with that, but he was getting the uneasy feeling that he was being manipulated. "Huh," he grunted.

"I think everybody should have six hugs a day," Christian went on.

"Well, that's hogwash," Ed said. "I can't remember the last time anybody hugged me, and I'm doing fine."

"Bub and Cate," Christian said.

"What about 'em?" Ed asked.

"They're your hugs."

"Hogwash," Ed said again, just as Bub and Cate came racing back from sniffing whatever they'd been sniffing and jumped up on Ed. Together, they knocked him over, walked on him, licked him, as if they hadn't seen him for ten years instead of ten minutes.

"Get off me, you mangy mutts," Ed told them, struggling to get away, but not too hard.

Well, they'd heard that before. They didn't pay any attention.

When Ed had righted himself and picked the

leaves out of his beard, he headed into the pink-crystal room, the one he used for his office, trailed by Christian and the dogs.

"I don't have time for this nonsense," he said stiffly, hoping the whole problem would somehow go away if he didn't look at it. "I'm a very busy person, waging an important campaign, and my time is valuable."

"What important campaign?" Christian asked.

"I'm going to bust Mab's monopoly if it's the last thing I ever do."

"You mean *Queen* Mab?" Christian asked. "The Tooth Fairy?"

"Tooth Tyrant is more like it," Ed grumbled. "She's got more work than she can handle, even with that incompetent flock of flying assistants she's got, most of which couldn't read a map to save their lives—if she even has any decent maps, which I doubt."

He warmed to his subject, which had begun as yet another troll tradition—the one that says the highest achievement a troll should aspire to is to take on a special task that will benefit the greatest number of people (even if they are children)—and had become a crusade. Most of the reason that it had was because Mab's inefficiency was so outrageous, it just plain gave him the whim-whams.

Ed continued. "More than once I've seen them buzzing around in the forest, running into trees and dropping their little parcels of money. I'll bet there are plenty of kids who *never* get their lost teeth picked up. And there are plenty of others who get those printed messages about how her secretary's out sick so everything's backed up, or how bad weather caused flight delays, or whatever. The truth is, Mab's overwhelmed and she won't admit it. And she won't let go of any of the business, either. Monopoly's not good, you know. Makes an enterprise lazy and uncreative. I've got some good ideas. I could give her a run for her eyeteeth if I could just get a nose under the door. I'm very busy," he repeated.

After a pause Christian said quietly, "I could help you. I could learn to do things. I could probably even invent something that would make whatever you're doing easier."

"No way, José," Ed said. "Impossible. Out of the question. We're going to find your family. Trust me."

3

Well, they didn't. And all Chris could—or would—tell him was that his parents were named Mother and Father and that they lived in a big stone house, but he didn't know where it was. Ed had no clue about where to start looking. Travelers, wanderers, warriors, and creatures verging on extinction from all over the known world passed through these woods on their way from Hither to Yon, so Christian's family could be anybody from anywhere. And the hunting horns and bloodhounds never came back after that one day, so either they'd given up on finding Christian, or they'd moved their search to a more remote part of the forest. Ed had heard all about the dragons and ogres, monsters and witches who lived on the other side of the vast forest, as well as the sour-tempered and unreasonable King Beaufort, and he wasn't about to go over there and run into one of them.

Actually, having Chris around turned out to be a better arrangement than Ed had imagined. For one thing, he was a sweeter-natured child than their initial acquaintance would suggest. True, he could be stubborn, but usually about something that turned out to be justified, so Ed eventually decided his reasons for not wanting to go back to his family must be good ones. Furthermore, he could already read and write, and he was eager to help Ed write his hundreds of letters to the other members of the LEFT (Leprechauns, Elves, Fairies, and Trolls) Association advocating a breakup of Queen Mab's tooth fairy monopoly. At the LEFT Conference each year, there was a vote on this issue, and while Ed hadn't managed a winning campaign yet, he wasn't giving up. He had hundreds of years to pursue his cause. Sooner or later he had to be successful. Then the ODD (Outstanding Distinguished Deed) Medal would be his.

Chris was also a great companion for the dogs. He spent hours playing with them and teaching them tricks, something Ed didn't always have time or inclination for. The boy was good at entertaining himself, too: exploring, bringing back unusual plants—sometimes edible and other times only beautiful—reading the assortment of dropped books found in the forest, studying the stars through the collapsible telescope, and inventing things. He hadn't been kidding about being an inventor. Or about making a big mess when he was working on something. He built one peculiar contraption after another out of forest-found items— contraptions that looked as if they might have a purpose, just not one that Ed (or Christian) could identify.

ED NOTICED that Chris was spending more and more time on the promontory outside the cave, looking through the collapsible telescope at King Swithbert's castle on the bluffs across the wide, rushing river. The royal family spent a great deal of time on the broad, walled stone terrace at the bluff's edge, and Chris seemed to enjoy watching King Swithbert and Queen Olympia, their four little daughters, and their courtiers going about their business.

Without being sure he wanted to hear the answer, Ed said one day, "I notice you watch the royal family a lot. Do you miss your own family?"

Christian gave him a serious brown-eyed look. "I can hardly remember those people, and I'm sure I don't miss them. I like my new family. It's a lot more interesting."

"Yeah?" Ed asked, trying not to let his chest puff up. "You think so?"

"Yep," Chris said, raising the telescope to his eye again. "And more fun, too."

Ed bounced on his toes a few times and then cleared his throat. "Well. I guess I'd better go . . . do . . . uh . . . something interesting."

"Okay," Christian said absently. "See you later."

Christian had told Ed he couldn't remember his family, and he meant it. He'd tried hard to forget them. But little pictures appeared in his mind from time to time. Two babies in blue baskets. A woman's long white hands holding a deck of cards. A man's voice, strong and scary, telling him that it was difficult to believe his fairy birth-gift had been good luck when he was in trouble so much of the time. A fair-haired little girl running up a long flight of stone steps, chasing a fat puppy.

When Christian had these memories, he felt no deficiency or regret—only a distant curiosity followed by a rush of gratitude for Ed, Bub, Cate, the cave, and the forest. He never doubted that his escape had been sensible, though he suspected that it wouldn't be the last escape he ever made. All his life he'd had the feeling that he was headed toward something—something that felt big—but he didn't know what it was. Somehow, though, he knew that being with Ed and the dogs, wandering through the forest, working on his inventions, and watching the world across the river, was preparing him for it in a way that his previous life had not.

ONE NIGHT, after Christian had been with Ed for a year or so, while Ed was supervising Chris's bedtime routine, a realization came upon the troll with the impact and terror of a lightning strike: He was a *parent*!

"What's wrong?" Chris asked when Ed paused, thunderstruck, holding Christian's nightshirt out to him.

"Plenty," Ed said, handing over the nightshirt.

"Did I do something?" Chris asked, his brown eyes troubled.

"Not that I know about . . . yet," Ed said, not recognizing that he sounded like most of the parents in the world, saying words designed to nudge their kids onto the right side of disorderly conduct. "It's something I need to think about."

"Can I help you?" Chris asked, buttoning the shirt and rolling up the sleeves.

Ed's heart did a little pixie jig inside his chest. The sensation was strong enough to cause him to put his hand over the sensitive spot. This kid that he hadn't wanted in his life had just about taken it over. The old troll had lived a long time without anybody around to help him. He'd gotten used to that—so used to it that he'd never even noticed the absence. But now that the vacant spot had been filled, he couldn't think how he'd managed without this handsome little boy with his crazy inventions and his tricks for the dogs—how many people had dogs who could clear the dinner table and sing in harmony?—and his willingness, even eagerness, to participate in whatever Ed was doing.

"You always tell me not to use my shirttail to blow my nose," Christian said, watching Ed. "So how come you can do it?"

Ed dropped his shirttail and rubbed his eyes with the back of his hand. He had to be a role model, for pete's sake. "It was a sudden attack of hay fever," he said gruffly. "I won't be doing it again. After all, what's sauce for the goose is sauce for the eager beaver. You got that?"

"I don't know." Christian almost never understood Ed's sayings but somehow got the drift of them anyway. "Does it mean don't blow my nose on my shirttail?"

"Yeah. Now get in bed."

After Christian and the dogs were in bed, Ed plucked a book on etiquette from the green-crystal library. Heading back to the parlor, he could hear Bub and Cate softly yowling a harmonized lullaby in Chris's bedroom.

He settled himself in his easy chair by the fire and began to read. It was up to him to make sure that Christian grew up minding his p's and q's and r's and s's. And all the rest of the letters, too. And he'd better get up to speed on them himself, since he hadn't even known that burping at the table was punishable by being dragged off to your room by your ear.

Part Two

1

Eleven Years Later

Edric had just finished an excellent meal, prepared by Christian, of gopher goulash, artichoke hearts, spinach salad, and cherries jubilee. He burped contentedly. "Who do you suppose ever figured out that artichokes are edible?" he asked. "They look lethal."

"Me, probably," Christian answered as Bub and Cate removed the plates from the table that Christian had not only built but had equipped with a crank that lowered it to the dogs' level for easier clearing. "I've never heard of anybody eating them before us." Of course, how would he know? The world was a big place, and more and more, he was realizing how little of it he knew.

Ed shouldn't have been surprised that Chris had discovered artichokes were edible. The boy had always had a sense of adventure—and not until recently had it begun to concern Ed. Oh, it was fine as long as it only extended to the odd plants that only occasionally made them sick when they ate them. And Ed didn't mind Chris's strange inventions, some of which, unlike the ones from his childhood, actually worked. Like the elevator that brought water up the bluff to the cave from the river. Or the boomerang arrows that came back to him if he missed his target.

But lately Christian's explorations kept him gone longer than usual, his inventions were noisier and more complicated than ever, and his culinary concoctions had approached the seriously bizarre. (Even Bub and Cate had rejected the rutabaga parfaits.) And he was restless in a way that Ed unhappily suspected was normal for a young person bearing down hard on manhood. Which forced him to think about Christian's nonexistent social life.

The boy needed some friends besides an old troll and a bunch of animals. Oh, once in a while he had a conversation with Hayes Centaur or Claypool Sasquatch, the gamekeepers, or with a leprechaun or picnicker or elf, or one of Mab's cohorts passing through the forest, but that didn't amount to a hill of figs.

Ed wondered if it wasn't time to start trying again to find Christian's family. He knew it would be the right thing to do, even though Christian had made it clear he wasn't interested. But more and more he had to wonder if he'd postponed it too long. And if he couldn't locate Chris's family, maybe it was time to think about releasing him to find his own way in the world. Ed had to admit that the very thought of doing that gave him a lacerating pain right in the center of his heart.

He sighed and considered whether he should add a postscript to his letters. After he got through detailing all of Mab's failings, of course. He could kill one bird with two stones by also asking if the recipient of the letter knew anything about a little boy who had gone missing in the forest about twelve years before. Walter and Carrie, the carrier pigeons Chris had trained to deliver Ed's correspondence more efficiently than passing pilgrims, crusaders, gnomes, and gryphons could, wouldn't be happy about longer letters. But the etiquette book had stressed the importance of doing what you knew was right, even when it was inconvenient—even when you didn't want to do it at all.

CHRIS'S FAVORITE invention, for quite a while, had been a bigger, better telescope with which he could keep a closer eye on King Swithbert's court across the river.

He'd watched the four princesses—the beautiful blond triplets and the smaller, darker younger one—grow up. He'd been an unseen guest at the masked balls, and the summer picnics on the terrace, and the triplets' triple wedding. He'd watched old King Swithbert get even older, and Queen Olympia get that cross little line between her eyebrows and that dissatisfied pout to her mouth. And while he watched them, he felt that now-familiar odd stirring, that sensation of something coming—something *bigger*, something *other*. And increasingly, the sense that he no longer fit so well where he was.

"I THINK I'LL go outside for a while," Christian said one evening, after he'd tidied up the kitchen. "Before the sun sets. I love these long twilights."

"Okay by me," Ed said, turning to his relentless correspondence. The annual LEFT Conference was coming up soon, and once again he was vigorously trying to drum up support for getting Mab to let go of some of the tooth fairy business. Everybody knew she was past her prime by a good hundred years but still hanging on like grim death to a business she hadn't managed well for as long as anyone could remember.

Why, he bet she didn't collect a quarter of the teeth on the first night they were placed under the pillow. Some, he knew, she didn't get to until the third or fourth night. And then she was inconsistent in what she paid for them—sometimes a lot, sometimes a pittance. She said she used the little teeth to make crowns for her fairies, but that was a can of baloney if Ed had ever heard any. What she did was toss them into storerooms, where they gradually lost their pearly luster and crumbled into chalky dust by the bushel. Anybody with an ounce of sense knew that teeth, like people, had to be kept in use to maintain their zip.

If Ed had his way, he'd build a palace from them. Imagine the radiance of it, all those little burnished white bricks softly glowing. He'd keep his palace polished with toothpaste so it always gleamed, and he'd stud it with the colored crystals that made up his cave and were so common in this part of the forest that they could sometimes be found lying on the ground like ordinary rocks.

He went to the mouth of the cave and looked out at the dwindling colors of the summer day. He was a lucky troll, and he knew it. None of his brothers had found as splendid a cave as he had, or had it as good as he did, or was on as promising a track toward the ODD Medal. He would soon be at the LEFT Conference listening to them complain about their lots. Ed sighed and went back to his letter writing.

CHRISTIAN SAT on a rock by the top of a waterfall that ricocheted, in sparkling segments, off the boulders and into the river below. Directly opposite, far across the river, was the castle he never tired of watching. He'd seen how the beautiful golden-haired triplets had spent most of their time together in an extravaganza of pastel femininity while their little sister spent most of her time in solitary pursuits: reading, cultivating pots of flowering plants, playing with her three small dogs. It took him years to realize it, but he finally saw that, shortly after he'd come to live with Ed, people had quit touching the dark-haired sister—they even seemed to go out of their way to avoid it. Old King Swithbert was the only one who ever did touch her, patting her absentmindedly in passing, holding her arm for support as he took his slow constitutional back and forth across the terrace. If Christian had ever seen anybody in need of six hugs a day—or even one—that dark-haired princess was the one.

He extended the telescope and focused it on the terrace. The princess sat alone in a plain wooden chair, reading. He tried to focus on the title, but she kept tilting the book to catch the failing light, so he couldn't see the cover. Her thick shining curls were caught untidily back in a silver cord, but she wore no jewelry. Her second-best everyday crown—he knew them all by now—hung on the back of the chair where she could grab it and clap it on her head if her mother, who seemed excessively concerned with her own and everyone else's wardrobes, appeared. He'd seen her do it dozens of times, and it always made him smile, the way she slung that emerald-studded thing around as if it were Ed's old woolen cap.

Littered around her chair were dog toys, a cup and saucer, several books, a shawl, and a watering can. That homey mess made her seem like a regular person, and not a princess at all.

The most royal he'd ever seen her was three years back, at her sisters' outdoor wedding. In her full regal regalia, she'd looked pretty spectacular to him— sparkling with diamonds, aflutter with lace and ribbons, squirming and scratching at her unaccustomed finery. He knew what that was like. He'd never forgotten that hot, irritating blue velvet suit. He was much more comfortable in the mismatched forest-found clothing that he wore now.

Struck by a sudden thought, he rushed back to the

cave, grabbed a piece of Ed's stationery, scrawled a few words on it, and woke Walter up from his perch. Walter squawked grouchily.

"Hey," Ed said, "what's that all about? Walter needs his rest. He's got a lot of mail to deliver tomorrow." The metal cylinders that attached to the pigeons' legs were big enough for only a small slip of paper with three lines of writing, so Walter and Carrie had to make many trips to deliver all of Ed's missives, even if he wrote his tiniest.

"He's not going far," Christian said. "Just one trip across the river." And he rushed out again.

Well, Ed had been wondering when something like this would happen. He knew who Christian was watching through that telescope. He'd tried to be a good parent, emphasizing that honest toil was the route to success, insisting on regular brushing and flossing, teaching every single manner in the etiquette book, even though Christian would never need most of them—"Good day, Your Grace" was the way to greet a duke; the oyster fork was the one with the three little tines; never be late to the opera. Yet somehow he'd never gotten around to any discussion about girls. Women. The opposite sex. For pete's sake, how could he discuss them when he didn't even know what to call them? Besides, his own love life wasn't anything to blow your horn home about. He admired the same red-haired troll maiden every year at the LEFT Conference and still, after all these decades, had never gotten up the nerve to speak to her.

Ed sighed. Now he'd have to stand by while the boy got his heart broken, and he wasn't looking forward to that. A princess, even a plain, unpopular one, wasn't going to give Christian the time of day, you could bet your bottom doubloon on that.

CHRISTIAN ROLLED his message into the metal cylinder and attached it to Walter's leg. He didn't know why he hadn't thought of this before. It's what carrier pigeons were meant for—and if the technology existed, he was a fool not to use it. How much harder communication had been before p-mail.

He told Walter where to go, released him out over the waterfall, and scurried to hide behind a bush, where he watched through the telescope.

It seemed to take Walter forever to cross the river, but finally he fluttered to a halt on the arm of the girl's chair. Absently, without looking up from her book, she tried to push him away with her elbow. Walter squawked and stayed where he was. She tried again, and again he squawked. This time she looked up. He stuck out his leg. She hesitated, looked quickly around, and then unhooked the cylinder, read the message, and hurried inside. Walter flew along beside her; he'd been trained not to leave until the cylinder had been reattached to his leg, preferably with a return message in it. Walter could make a terrible nuisance of himself. It was Ed's way of getting prompt answers.

Oh, man, Christian thought. Ed's going to kill me if we never get Walter back. What was I thinking? She could have a dragoon of castle guards over here in the morning to hunt me down.

As it so often does, an impulsive, daring act suddenly—and too late—seemed seriously flawed in its conception and in its inability to be retracted.

But the princess returned in a few minutes, Walter in her arms. She took him to the terrace wall and flung him out into the darkening sky. As he flew away, she leaned forward, squinting, trying to follow his flight. Even after Walter had landed in the bushes on his side of the river, Christian could still make her out, leaning over the wall, her pale yellow gown glowing faintly in the dusk.

Christian hustled Walter back into the cave, snapped the cylinder off his leg, and popped him onto the perch next to Carrie. Walter gave Christian a baleful look, fretfully settled his feathers, and tucked his head beneath his wing. All the while Ed bent over his letters, giving furtive glances from under his shaggy eyebrows as Christian opened the cylinder, extracted the message, and read it.

He looked up at Ed. "She's reading Greek myths. I asked her what she was reading and she told me. Greek myths. We have those, too! I've read them a bunch of times. And she signed her name. At last I know her name."

"Well, what is it?" Ed asked with resignation. For some reason he was remembering King Louis the Stammerer, who had died on horseback while chasing a girl who'd run into her house, splitting his head open on the lintel of the door. Ed always wondered if that was because he hadn't been able to say "W-w-w-whoa" in time. What had happened to King Louis supplied plenty of evidence about how dangerous getting interested in a girl could be.

"Marigold. Isn't that a pretty name? Marigold." His eyes on Marigold's tiny letter, Christian left the room in search of the book of Greek myths.

Now why'd she have to go and answer him? Ed wondered. Is she just going to play games with him before she breaks his heart, the way a cat will toy with a mouse? That's about what he'd expect a princess to be: heartless and scheming.

2

Christian sat up late rereading the myths, and with every one that he finished, he framed a new letter to Marigold in his mind. He wanted to ask her—well, to tell the truth, he wanted to ask her everything.

When he finally blew out his candle and lay down on the furs with Bub and Cate, he couldn't sleep. He'd never felt the way he felt tonight—all tingly and fizzy, as if he'd had a spell cast upon him. He hoped he wasn't coming down with something.

Walter and Carrie were busy all the next few days carrying Ed's lengthy missives here and there. They were too exhausted by the end of each day to make even the short trip across the river. Christian was beside himself, wanting to send another message to Marigold and not being able to do so.

All he could do was watch her. She seemed the same as ever, tending her flowers on the terrace, reading, playing with her dogs, walking with her father, acting as if being royalty was nothing special. *She* wasn't all tingly and fizzy, though she did seem more interested than usual in the birds that flew over the terrace.

One morning Chris got up extra early, while Ed was still conked out on his bed of furs, snoring loudly enough to make the purple crystals on the ceiling of his bedroom shiver and chime faintly. Walter was awake on his perch, busily preening himself. So much mail delivery gave him little time for personal grooming, and he was vain enough that that bothered him.

Christian had already written his message and put it into a cylinder. All he had to do now was get it onto Walter's leg.

"Hey, Walter. Good morning. Nice morning for a short warm-up flight, isn't it?"

Walter gave him a suspicious, beady-eyed look.

"Just across the river. To . . . to Marigold." Merely saying her name made him feel happy. And, even though he knew he should think of her as *Princess* Marigold, he wanted to call her just plain Marigold.

Walter sighed heavily as Christian clipped the

cylinder to his leg. "I told her I read Greek myths, too. I told her my favorite is about Jason and the Argonauts and all their adventures. Even though it has a sad ending, it's exciting up until then. And Jason grew up in a cave, away from his original home, too."

Christian had watched Walter take off before he realized that it was way too early for anybody at the castle to be up, and Walter would have to hang around on the terrace, maybe for hours, before Marigold appeared. Oh, what a knucklehead he was. Way too stupid to be corresponding with a princess. Christian felt his lack of worldly knowledge more than ever. He might know how to address a duke or recognize an oyster fork, but he had no clue whatsoever about what went on between human males and females.

Through the telescope he followed Walter's progress. The sun was still below the horizon, but the sky had that magical deep lavender opalescence of a high-summer day that was going to be a scorcher—but later. For now all was still and pearly and perfect.

And to make it more perfect, just then Marigold, wearing something gauzy and flowing, stepped onto the terrace, yawning and stretching. She leaned on the wall, looking across the river just as Walter landed by her right elbow. He held the leg with the cylinder out to her in a long-suffering manner, but she just smiled at him and unclipped it. She read the message, smiled bigger, and held one finger up to him, signaling him to wait.

When she came back, she had paper, pen, ink, and a handful of grain she scattered along the terrace wall for Walter to peck at while she pondered her answer. Mollified, he enjoyed his breakfast as she wrote three lines, waited for the ink to dry, then clipped the cylinder onto his leg. He finished the last of the grain and flapped off.

Christian hid in the bushes so Marigold couldn't see where Walter delivered the message. After Chris unclipped the cylinder, Walter headed back inside, but not before executing a few carefree loop-the-loops in pure pleasure over having had a hearty breakfast and an easy job accomplished on a splendid summer morning.

Christian took one more quick look through the telescope. Just then Queen Olympia emerged onto the terrace in her full satin-dress-and-pearl-tiara regalia, with some kind of fur piece draped over one arm. She found Marigold, in what apparently was her nightie, gazing off across the river. Christian couldn't hear what the queen was saying, of course, but there was no mistaking that a scolding was taking place. Marigold stood, casting her eyes slightly above Olympia's head, looking like a thundercloud with a clamped-shut mouth.

She almost quivered with the effort not to talk back to her mother, though Christian was sure that Queen Olympia deserved a little back talk. He'd seen plenty of the way she bossed everybody around—including King Swithbert. He had to admire Marigold's self-control. Bursting out with angry words was always so much easier than maintaining one's dignity and self-respect. But not reacting often had the satisfying side effect of further enraging the person who was giving you trouble. That's what Ed's etiquette book said, though Chris had had no personal experience with such things. Just as he'd had no personal experience with just about everything—something that was becoming more of a consideration for him every day.

The first thing he wanted to do now—whether the etiquette book would like it or not—was to run over there and stick up for Marigold. What was so bad about wanting to see the sunrise in your nightie?

Christian watched Marigold until she and her mother went inside. Then he opened her note:

Do you know the story of Andromeda?

He knew he should, but there were so many of them, he couldn't remember which one that was. He ran back to the cave and flipped madly through the pages of his Greek myth book until he found it. Then he remembered Andromeda was the daughter of a vain queen who had angered Poseidon, the sea god, so much that he sent a sea monster to devour her kingdom. To save the kingdom, the king had to sacrifice Andromeda to the monster. Chained to a cliff she called on her fiancé, a prince, to rescue her, but he was too cowardly. Perseus, a poor humble youth who didn't know he was really the son of the god Zeus, showed up just in time to slay the monster. After that he and Andromeda lived happily evermore. And when they died, Zeus put them into the sky as constellations so they could be together always. There was a drawing that showed which stars were Perseus and Andromeda.

And of course, Christian recognized those constellations. He'd seen them through his telescope.

Did Marigold feel she was being sacrificed to her mother's vanity? Did she need to be rescued? Who was the monster? Was there a fiancé? Christian's mind spun with dramatic possibilities.

Or maybe Andromeda's myth was just a nice story with a happy ending and that's why Marigold liked it. Maybe she was shallow and stupid and he'd hate her if they ever met. What could you really tell about somebody from a couple of p-mails?

The answer, it seemed to him, was to send more p-mails, to get to know more about her. To find out why she liked the story.

He waited until he saw her alone again on the terrace, now wearing a proper morning dress. Message in hand, he ran to the cave, hijacking Carrie from Ed just as he was about to snap her cylinder on. "Hey!" Ed yelled as Christian grabbed the pigeon. Carrie squawked, too, but Chris hustled her out to the waterfall and sent her across the river.

It turned out that Marigold liked the myth because she loved watching the stars and liked knowing their stories. But Christian thought there was more to it than that.

He wished he could ask her. Because he felt instinctively that asking her about that would be too personal and intrusive, he decided to ask her about other things. Like when her birthday was. He wanted to know where she belonged in the zodiac.

And that was how their long p-mail correspondence began.

April 19. I'm 17. I'm an Aries. Why did you decide to write to me?

—Marigold

You seemed so absorbed in your book. I
wanted to know what you were reading.

—C.

For some reason, he was reluctant to tell her his name. The more anonymous he stayed, the bolder he felt—as if he were someone else, an alternate version of himself, a version who casually corresponded with a princess. A version who couldn't tell her his own birthday because he didn't know it.

You can see me?

—Marigold

P.S. What does C. stand for?

He thought her first question sounded a bit alarmed, as most people would be if they found out they were being watched. But the fact that she'd added a P.S. meant she was curious about him, which he took as a good sign. He debated for a long time about how to answer.

Sometimes I can see you. C. stands for my
name.

He knew he was being tricky and evasive, but he *could* see her only sometimes. He couldn't see her if she wasn't on the terrace. He couldn't see her at night even if she was. He knew the thing about his name might be sort of irritating, too, but he wasn't ready to tell her his real name—he liked being his alternate, bolder self—and he didn't want to lie to her ever.

She sent the pigeon back with an empty cylinder that time, so he knew she had backbone. But he wasn't at all glad that might be the last thing he'd ever find out about her. He waited a few days, brooding and grumpy, and then shanghaied both birds and four cylinders for a try at an apology.

> I'm sorry. I can see you from afar with my telescope. I'm shy about telling you my name.
>
> Besides, using C. instead of my whole name saves space for other things I want to write to you about. Okay?
>
> Can't we leave it at C. for a while? It's a perfectly ordinary name, anyway.

I didn't mean to sound smart-alecky. I
hope you'll write back. You are such a
good correspondent.　　　　　—C.

To Chris's great relief, Carrie came back with a message.

Charlemagne? Crispin? Colin? Cosmo?
Christian? Chauncey?　　　　—Marigold

He told her she'd guessed his name, but he didn't tell her which one it was.

Charlemagne: Can you see the stars with
your telescope? Can you see Perseus and
Andromeda? I envy them.

P.S. I know that one time out of six I'll
have your name right.　　　—Marigold

Why do you envy them?　　　　—C.

He couldn't think of anything else he wanted to know just then.

Crispin: Because they had a grand
adventure together, and because they knew
great love and because they were each

other's companions and best friends
and bulwarks.   —M.

He had to look up *bulwark* in the dictionary that
Ed had found in the forest just a few days before.
It meant (1) a defensive wall or rampart and (2) any
safeguard or defense; anything that protects or shel-
ters. Suddenly he wanted to have a bulwark, a protection and shelter—other than Ed, that is. And he
wanted to be one for someone else.

Colin: Has anybody ever tried to marry
you off? What did you do about it?

                              —M.

No. But here's what I would do if they
did—be as unpleasant and as undesirable
as possible.

                              —C.

*Christian: You're a genius! It worked! I
picked my nose and didn't brush my hair
and wiped my hands on Flopsy, one of*

*my dogs, after I ate. That boring suitor
left in a hurry after dinner.   —M.*

Christian loved that this message had his name on it. And he laughed when she told him what she'd done. But he suspected that this wouldn't be the last suitor to show up. He'd seen how Queen Olympia had paraded suitors through for the triplets, and he knew that scoldings would follow whenever Marigold scared away any of her parade.

*Cosmo: As punishment my mother says I
must pick out all the bollixed-up ladies-
in-waiting embroidery. I <u>hate</u> that.   —M.*

*Marigold: When I have to do something I
hate, I whistle. Then at least my mouth is
happy.   —C.*

It gave him a funny feeling in his stomach to think about her mouth.

*Chauncey: I tried the whistling, which
drove Mother absolutely <u>mad</u>. She says it's
undignified and unladylike. I'll use it on*

*the next suitor. He arrives next week. I
don't want to be dignified or ladylike
for him.*   —M.

*Marigold: How do you know? Maybe you'll
like him.*   —C.

Christian hated to even suggest this, but he needed
to know how she could be so sure she'd want to drive
him away.

*Colin: I don't want to marry anybody who
thinks of me only as a dowry and an
alliance instead of a partner and a best*

*friend. Royal marriages are arrangements,
not love matches. Except for my sisters,
who are lucky in everything.*   —M.

He wanted to tell her that if she needed a best
friend, he could be it. But of course he didn't. No

matter how bold his other self might feel, he was still a forest commoner and she was a princess.

Charlemagne: Whistling worked, but I can't use it again. My punishment this time is 3 hours a day at the harpsichord—

she can hear if I stop. I have to play the same tune all 3 hours. Can you hear me?
                                                        —M.

He tried. He whipped up an ear trumpet from random items in one of the storage rooms and, once in a while, thought he heard a few tinkling notes above the sound of the river. But maybe he was only imagining it.

3

Colin: *Where do you live? What is your family like? Do you have pets? What's your favorite thing to eat? Can you swim? Can*

you ice-skate? I've never been out of this castle. What is the world like? —M.

What a lot of questions! He could answer all but the last one. He lay awake that night thinking that he knew almost as little about the world as she did, even if he could swim and ice-skate and eat artichokes and invent things and harmonize with his dogs.

> *Marigold: I live in a cave with my foster*
> *father*

It had taken him a long time to decide how to describe Ed.

> *and two great dogs who can sing. I*
> *can swim and ice-skate and I love*

> *artichokes. The world is . . . big. And*
> *complicated.*

He took a deep breath and added:

> *And I wish we could explore*
> *it together.*   —C.

Walter came back with empty cylinders that time.

Oh no, Christian thought. I've offended her. She probably thinks I'm one of those gold-digging princes who keep coming around.

He waited a few days, then sent a message.

> *Marigold: Have I offended you?*
> *   —C.*

57

This time Walter came back loaded.

Christian: I must tell you that I have a
curse on me. Maybe you won't want to be
my friend now, but I had to tell you.

Only I have the power to break the curse, and
I have to discover how to do it by myself.
And nothing I've tried has worked.   —M.

Christian prepared both pigeons to send so that
Marigold could write twelve lines instead of six.

Marigold: Is that why no one touches you?
—C.

C: It was not meant to be a curse. It was my
fairy birth-gift—the gift of sensitivity to
the thoughts and feelings of others. But my

birth fairy overdid it. I can actually <u>know</u>
other people's thoughts—but only if I'm
touching them. Most people don't want me

to know what they're thinking. Which is

scary, isn't it? So I have no friends except
my dogs and my old father. So I'll under-

stand if you don't want to explore the
world with me. Even if such a thing were
possible. —M.

There wasn't a single thought in his head that he
didn't want her to know about.

Marigold: I'm not afraid to have you
know my thoughts. Isn't that what best
friends do? —C.

He watched through the telescope while she read
that one, and felt a tremor in his heart when she put
her head down on her folded arms and wept. Carrie
stood by on the parapet, her little birdie head cocked
quizzically.

C: Since there's no possibility that you'll
ever be able to touch me, maybe we can be
best friends. How do we do that? —*Marigold*

Well, Christian was at a loss about how to answer
her. But he knew that knights made pledges of loyalty

and honor, which they defended with their lives, and that was exactly what he felt like doing with Marigold.

> *Marigold: I think we should make a promise*
> *to each other about our friendship and seal it*
> *by exchanging something important to us—*
>
> *a treasure we want the other one to have. A*
> *<u>little</u> treasure, so the pigeons can carry it.*
>
> —C.

> *C: That's a wonderful idea. I pledge to*
> *share with you my thoughts, my sorrows,*
> *my joys, and never to lie or deceive. And*
>
> *I pledge always to listen to you and give*
> *help and comfort and companionship.* —M.

There was no treasure in the cylinder, but knotted around Carrie's neck was a fine linen handkerchief with a gold *M* embroidered in the corner. And tied into it was a single diamond earring. Christian was shocked by this gift. He'd had in mind something more sentimental—a childhood toy, a favorite quotation from a book, a secret. He had nothing this special to give her. And he wondered if he could come up with a pledge of friendship as complete and as touching as hers. It made him think about how very important and also demanding friendship is. Finally he wrote:

> Marigold: I can't make a better pledge than
> yours, so I promise the same. And I'm
> sending you a crystal from the ceiling
>
> of my bedroom—the first place I ever felt
> completely safe and happy.   —C.

> C: I sent you one of the earrings my father
> gave me when I was born. It represents every-
> thing I know about loyalty and trustworthiness
>
> and devotion. He's getting a little dotty now,
> but he's still the best person I know. And the
> only one who lets me touch him. Does

Christian had to send Walter right back to get the rest of the message. And he was happy to know that the gift she had given him was even more sentimental and special than he'd realized.

your foster father touch you?   —Marigold

Chris had to stop and think. Ed and the dogs were so much a part of him that he wasn't always sure where he left off and they began—especially the dogs, who were so often in his bed or his lap or his way. But, yes, now that he thought of it, Ed touched him all the time. A comradely clasp on the shoulder, or a friendly punch in the arm, or a good-night hug. In the beginning Ed had touched him only when necessary, to help him bathe or dress. But he remembered vividly the first time Ed had touched him with affection.

They'd been out in the woods, gathering dropped and discarded items, when Christian had heard a whir like hummingbird wings. He looked up to see a tiny fairy hovering in the air between him and Ed, her wings going so fast they were a blur. She wore a gauzy iridescent gown with an ink stain on the bodice, a minute crown cocked over one ear, and a couple of pencils stuck in the knot of her hair.

"Oh, it's you," Ed said.

"Yes, it's me," the fairy snapped. "And I'm telling

you, if you don't lay off this campaign of yours, you're going to be sorry."

"Oh yeah?" Ed said pugnaciously. "What are you going to do? Tickle me to death?"

"I'll report you to the LEFT disciplinary board. I'll have you banned from the conferences."

"Oh, get a grasp, Mab. You can't do that. There's no rule against campaigning for honest competition. If you were doing your job, I wouldn't be getting the kind of support I am."

She snorted daintily. "You have no idea what's involved in running an operation like mine."

"You don't either, apparently," Ed said. "I'll bet you're lost right now."

"Don't be ridiculous." Mab sniffed. She pointed her wand at Christian and abruptly changed the subject. "Who's this?"

Ed came to stand behind Christian, though he was only slightly taller than the boy, and crossed his arms protectively over Chris's chest. "This is my . . . boy," Ed said. "He's staying with me." Ed tightened his hold, and as he did, Chris felt totally safe. Ed's arms around him were the best shelter and protection he had ever experienced—better than any number of high walls or locked doors or moats. He relaxed slightly, leaning back against Ed.

Maybe that's how Marigold felt about her father, too.

It had turned out Queen Mab *was* lost. They kept running into her for the rest of the afternoon as she blundered around, trying to find her way home while pretending she knew exactly where she was.

AFTER CHRISTIAN and Marigold decided to be best friends, they tried to communicate every day. Sometimes they could p-mail several times a day. Sometimes, when the weather was bad or Ed was in one of his writing frenzies, they had to wait days between messages. Christian hoped she felt as tortured by this as he did.

At least once a week Marigold sent him a joke. They were all awful. Clearly she needed to get out more so she could learn some better ones.

> C: *What fairy tale is about a beautiful girl who bakes bread?*
> <u>*Beauty and the Yeast*</u>.   —*Marigold*

> C: *Why don't people like Pinocchio?*
> *Because he's a little stiff and has a wooden smile.*   —*Marigold*

C: How did King Arthur read at night?
With a knight light.   —Marigold

C: What kind of music does a dragon
play?
Scales.   —Marigold. (I love this one.)

C: Can the Three Little Pigs keep a secret?
No. They squeal.   —Marigold

C: What two things can't a giant eat for
dinner?
Breakfast and lunch.   —Marigold

C: What do you get when a giant sneezes?
Out of the way.   —Marigold

Marigold: Where are you getting these
jokes?   —C.

C: From the stable boy who feeds the
unicorns. Don't you like them?
          —Marigold

*Marigold: I'm only telling you this because
I'm your best friend, but they're terrible.
Here's a good joke:*

*Have your eyes ever been checked?
No. They've always been brown.* —C.

Claypool Sasquatch had told him that joke, and it was even funnier because Claypool's eyes *were* checked.

Marigold's next message had a bit of a huffy tone to it.

*C: Well, it was funny, but not any funnier
than mine. Tell me another one.*
—*Marigold*

*Marigold: Did you know that if Minnehaha
married Santa Claus, she would be known
as Minnehaha Hoho?* —C.

*C: I don't think yours are any better than
mine.* —*Marigold*

So they had to agree to disagree about jokes. The only one they both liked was: Can you get fur from a skunk? Yes—as fur as possible.

He wished he could hear what her laugh sounded like.

AWFUL JOKES aside, Christian found that he and Marigold had much in common. She liked to watch the sunrise and the sunset, just as he did. And as he also did, she read everything—not just the few books her mother thought were proper but ones various visitors to the castle brought from all over the world, even if she had to hide them inside fake covers. He learned that she missed her sisters since they'd gotten married, even though she felt that she'd never gotten to know them very well. That her three little dogs were the best listeners in the whole castle. So good that she couldn't even pretend to be angry at them when they chased Fenleigh, her mother's pet ferret (which Chris had thought was a fur piece always draped over Olympia's arm). That she worried about her father's health. That she made perfumes from the flowers she grew in the terrace pots. That she had been forgotten by the Tooth Fairy more than once. That she wished she could live in a place where there weren't so many silly rules, like having to wear your crown all the time, and not talking to anybody who wasn't your same rank—how many royals were there, after all, that she could talk to?—and being required to attend so many boring lectures because her mother thought it was instructive (though Queen Olympia usually found a reason she herself couldn't attend). That, because she had never been allowed out of the castle, she was curious about everything.

In one message that touched him especially, she wrote:

> C: Do you ever feel as if you're in the
> wrong place, even if it's a nice place? As if
> you somehow don't fit, even if you try
>
> hard to? But how do you find your right
> place? Who can you ask?
> —Marigold

He had to think for a long time before he answered.

> Marigold: Yes, I have felt that way. Do you
> suppose everyone does? Or just us? I wish I
> knew how to find our right places.

Just keep looking, I suppose. I'm sorry I'm
no help.   —C.

C: You are always a help, just to know you're
there to tell such things to. But how can I
look when I must stay here?   —Marigold

Marigold:

All he wanted to write was her name again and
again. But he had to do more, had to be a best friend
and a bulwark.

Maybe you won't have to
be there forever. Maybe something will
change. But I don't know what.   —C.

In the next few messages, both of them sensed the
false cheerfulness that came from trying to reassure
the other in the face of real doubts. But they each
were still glad they had someone to be falsely cheerful
for.

4

On another high-summer day, a year later, Christian took his bow and arrow and headed out. They'd had meatless dinners for the past three nights, and though Christian didn't mind, Ed was sick of them. And Bub and Cate were craving squirrel knuckles. Tonight there had to be major protein for supper.

He was sitting silently on a stump, waiting for some big animal to come unsuspectingly along, when he heard the sound of hooves in the brush. He stood up, holding his bow. A deer? A moose? The king's guards?

It was Hayes Centaur, King Swithbert's game-keeper, patrolling the king's woods for poachers.

"Hey there," Hayes said when he saw Christian. "You wouldn't be planning to plug any of the king's animals with that thing, would you?"

Christian looked down at the bow in his hand. "Certainly not. Just a little target practice. On trees. For self-defense. You never know when you'll need it. Pays to keep sharp."

Chris was always glad to see the centaur—even at the risk of being caught poaching—because Hayes was such a talker, always full of news and opinions, bringing information from the bigger world that Chris was so curious about.

"I'm ready for a rest," Hayes said. "I've been out here since early this morning getting enough meat for the big doings at the castle tomorrow night."

"Big doings? What's going on?"

"Oh, it's another one of those get-the-princess-married-off dinners. Some prince comes over to check her out, talk about dowries, have a look at her jewels, all that."

"Oh," Christian said dejectedly. Marigold hadn't mentioned this one. And he always feared she would decide that one of these suitors made a better best friend than he did.

Hayes shrugged. "They always go away and don't come back. It's true she's no beauty, but she's loaded, and the queen makes the dowry bigger for each suitor. All I can figure is the princess must say something pretty bad to them or act crazy or something like that. She's always been nice enough to me, but everybody's got another side."

"I guess so," Christian said, trying not to laugh as he thought about how well Marigold had been using his advice to scare off suitors.

"Those sisters of hers—pretty as pictures, all that golden hair and hourglass figures and fancy manners. No problem finding husbands for those three. They didn't even have to open their mouths."

"Why is it so important for them all to get married?"

"Oh, that's Queen Olympia for you. Says she wants them to have the pleasure of their own homes. But if you ask me, it's because she wants to be the only royal dame in the castle. She's not one who likes to share the spotlight—unless it's with that pampered ferret of hers, the only one who ever gets a kind word from her. Besides, the king's getting on, you know, and if he kicks off before the princess gets married, Marigold becomes queen and Queen Olympia gets shuffled off to be the old royal dowager with no power. But if the princess is married when he goes off to his reward and is queen of some other kingdom,

Queen Olympia gets to be the ruler. I'm just guessing, but I think she'd really like that."

"So who's the suitor tonight?" Christian asked.

"Tonight there are two. One's that guy from Upper Lower Grevania, the one who's always shopping for a bride but never actually picking one. If you ask me, I think he just likes being an honored guest at all those castles. The other one is some distant shirttail relative of King Swithbert's who has no kingdom of his own. Which means he'd live here at the castle if the princess married him. Then she'd be married and still get to be the queen someday, which would please the old man. I venture to say, Queen Olympia would not be in favor of that plan."

"It doesn't sound as if either one of them is a very good candidate."

"Maybe not. But they're about the last choices, and Olympia wants to get it done. And the king is old-fashioned enough to think the princess would be happier if she had a spouse, though he should know better than that, being married to Olympia and all."

"What about the princess?" Christian asked. "What does she want?"

"Who knows? I'm not exactly her best friend. All I can say is, she seems pretty satisfied as is. She reads a lot and takes walks with her dad and teaches tricks to her dogs and makes these great perfumes that have really improved the atmosphere around the castle. Bathing's not everybody's favorite thing, you know. Of course, on the other hand, she's got that curse, and she's not allowed to leave the castle, and she's always in trouble with the queen about something. But it'd be my guess that nobody's ever asked her what she wants. The way royalty works, it probably doesn't matter."

Those words struck Christian like a blow. He wanted what Marigold desired to matter more than anything in the world.

"Well, I'd better get going," Hayes said. "The cooks'll be wanting to get started." He took a cloth bag from among the ones tied to his back and handed it to Christian. "I got a couple of extra rabbits here if you think you can do anything with them. And take the squirrel knuckles, too, since nobody I know has any use for them."

Christian took the bag. "You sure you don't need them?"

"Who do you think is going to need some squirrel knuckles? Or miss a couple of rabbits, with all the roast boars and suckling pigs and haunches of venison laid out for these guys? You given any more thought to coming to the castle for a steady job?" Every few months Hayes suggested Chris should apply for a job at the castle. Hayes thought everybody he liked should work there, where he could see them every day.

"Maybe," Christian said, surprising himself. The urge to experience more of the world was growing stronger daily, though leaving Ed and the dogs was almost too hard to think about. "If I wanted one, who should I talk to?"

"Mrs. Clover, the housekeeper. She'll fix you right up. Now I've got to get going."

"See you later." Christian lifted his hand in farewell and headed for home, supper in the cloth sack and a lot on his mind.

ED WAITED until the rabbit *au vin* was under his belt that evening to talk to Christian about the future, a talk he'd put off far too long. He knew all about the p-mailing with Marigold—he wasn't *blind*—which made this conversation all the more necessary. Chris needed to get a life, a real one that didn't involve futile fantasies about a princess.

"Sit down, Chris," Ed said. "I need to talk to you."

"What's wrong?" The tone of Ed's voice worried Christian. He pulled the dogs against him on either side, as if to form a shield against bad news.

Ed sighed. "This will be hard for both of us, but sometimes you just have to take the bear by the horns."

"Bull," Christian said.

"No, it's not," Ed said. "It's the dead truth."

"*Bull* by the horns," Christian said. "Not bear." He'd recently heard Hayes use that phrase and knew Ed must have it wrong. Bears didn't *have* horns.

"Oh. Well, here's what I've been thinking about. You're a young man now, and this is no kind of life for you, living buried in a cave with no friends."

In spite of the fact that he'd been thinking practically the same thing lately, Christian felt moved to say, "But I have you. And Bub and Cate and Walter and Carrie." Even as he said the words, he knew that wasn't enough for him now.

"That's too little," Ed said, wishing he didn't know it was true. "You need more. You're grown-up now, and you need to know more about the world. I'm starting to feel rotten about keeping you from it."

"But you haven't," Christian assured him. "I told you when I first got here I didn't want to go home. And I still don't."

"I'm not saying you have to go home." Especially since Ed didn't know where that was. None of his correspondents had had any helpful information about Christian's origins. "But I think you have to go *some-*

where. See what it's like to live around other people. Have a social life. You know."

Christian was quiet for a long time, and for once Ed was smart enough to keep his mouth shut and let him think. He'd have been pretty surprised if he'd known Christian had already made his decision and was just figuring out how to tell Ed.

But Ed could keep quiet only so long. He blurted, "If you don't like it out there, you know the door is always open to you." Because they lived in a cave, the door was always open to everyone, but neither of them mentioned that. They both knew what Ed meant.

Christian took a deep breath, but that did nothing to still his galloping heartbeat. "I think you're right," he said. "Hayes suggested again today that I try for a job at the castle. I'm going to take him up on it."

"At the castle? I was thinking you should get farther away. Really be on your own."

"Ed, I've never even been across the river. The castle might as well be the moon. Besides, I'd be close enough so we could p-mail if we wanted to." Not to mention that he'd be closer to Marigold, even though, as a commoner, he could never speak to her the way he did in his letters.

Ed saw nothing but trouble with this idea, what with Chris's useless interest in the princess and all. On the other hand, wasn't learning to deal with trouble part of what he wanted Christian to learn? Between Ed and the dogs, they'd protected Chris from just about everything while he was growing up. He'd never become a man if he didn't learn to solve his own problems. Ed just didn't want him to bite off more than he could swallow.

"Okay," he said. One of the first steps in letting go was allowing Chris to make his own decisions.

"I'll go tomorrow," Christian said, before lying down for a night so restless that both dogs finally gave up in a huff and went off to the yellow-crystal room, where they could get some sleep.

5

After breakfast Christian stood at the cave's entrance, all his worldly goods (one extra pair leather breeches, one extra shirt, two pairs underdrawers, one set shaving implements, one book Greek myths, one diamond earring wrapped in layers and layers of protective linen) tied into a bundle he carried in one hand. In the other he held his bow. His quiver of boomerang arrows was on his back, and his knife was on his belt.

Ed and the dogs stood facing him, as they had for the past ten minutes. Neither Christian nor Ed knew what to say, and the dogs gave each other puzzled looks at all this unmoving silence. Ed cleared his throat for the third time, but still no words came.

Christian took a deep breath and exhaled gustily.

Bub sat and Cate lay down.

Christian finally spoke. "I'll..." His voice cracked and he tried again. "I'll come see you on my first day off."

Ed nodded, for once speechless. He made an agreeing sound, though neither one of them knew if castle employees ever got a day off.

Christian moved his bow to the hand with the bundle and put his free hand on Ed's shoulder. "Thank you," he said. He gave Ed a quick, hard hug and turned away, walking fast into the trees.

The dogs scrambled up and ran after him, ignoring Ed's whistle calling them back. Why should they go back? They always went along with Christian on his rambles.

Ed's whistle got fainter until neither Christian nor the dogs could hear it. They were all glad of that; none of them wanted to be tempted to turn around, but for different reasons.

Christian stood on the bank of the wide, fast river waiting for the cyclops who piloted the ferry to notice him. Hayes had told him that this might take a while since one eye was only half as efficient as two.

The dogs sat beside him, ears up, anticipating another adventure.

Then Christian spotted the boat, upriver, coming straight across the water. A cable strung over the river kept the boat from drifting downstream in spite of the swift current. He set off along the riverbank to meet the boat. The dogs trotted along, tongues lolling, eyes bright.

"Need a lift?" the cyclops asked.

"Yes," Christian said.

"That'll be one silver."

Christian handed him the one silver coin he'd found in the forest long ago, aware that he couldn't come back across to see Ed unless he earned some money. As Ed would say, he'd buttered his bread and now he had to lie in it.

The cyclops squinted hard at the coin with his one eye before biting down hard on it and then putting it in his pocket.

The dogs tried to hop aboard, but Christian pushed them aside and told the boatman to cast off before they could get on again. Bewildered, Beelzebub barked himself hoarse—Christian could hear him even over the roar of the water—and would definitely be down with a sick headache all afternoon. Hecate threw herself about, howling and yowling in such a display of heartbroken abandonment that Christian had to believe she was sincere and not just emoting. Truthfully, if he didn't keep reminding himself of the adventure ahead of him, he might do the same thing.

He distracted himself by designing a better pulley system for the ferry cable. The cyclops was very impressed and said he would try it.

It was a long hike up to the castle from where the ferry landed, so Christian had plenty of time to wonder whether he was making a horrible mistake, trading the dull-but-comfortable known for the scary, unpredictable unknown. With each step his left foot took, he felt like a certifiable idiot to give up such a fine life with Ed. And with each step his right foot took, he felt exhilarated at the prospect of what surprises might lie ahead. But the decision was made. Without another silver coin, he wouldn't be going back across the river.

He crossed the drawbridge over the moat and presented himself to the guard at the portcullis.

"I'm here to see Mrs. Clover," he said. "About a position."

The guard, a true giant more than eight feet tall, laughed.

"A position, is it? Which position would that be?

Bent over so I can kick your backside? Or flat on your back after I've knocked you down?"

Christian couldn't think of one thing to say. It had been a very, very long time since anybody had said something unkind to him, but this guard's words made him remember exactly how it felt when that happened. And he had no doubt the giant could do anything he threatened.

But he bravely braced his shoulders and asked, "What's your name?"

"What do you care?" the guard responded. "You can just call me sir."

At that moment Hayes Centaur came clattering up the road and over the drawbridge.

"Hey!" Hayes said, catching sight of Christian. "Did you finally come for that job?"

"I'm trying," Christian said. "But I can't get past the front door."

"He's coming with me, Rollo," Hayes said to the guard. "Stop acting like such a————." He said a word Christian had never heard before but thought he wouldn't like to be called. "I don't want to have to report you to the queen. Come on, Chris."

So Christian followed Hayes—not his favorite end of a horse to be near—through the gates and into the inner bailey, knowing that he had already made an enemy.

MRS. CLOVER was plump and red-cheeked, with golden braids wound into a coronet, and she smelled like the plant she was named for. Christian wondered if her scent had been concocted by Marigold. Hayes handed a brace of partridges to Mrs. Clover to make stock for the soup.

Mrs. Clover took them and then turned to look at Christian. "And who is this handsome young man?"

"Oh," Hayes said, "this is Christian from the forest. He needs a job, and as I know you always have your eye out for a good squire, I thought maybe you could help him."

"I know just where he can be useful. You come along with me, young man. I'll outfit you with some livery and put you to work. It's all your meals, you sleep in the stables, and one piece of silver a week. Does that suit you?"

"Suits me quite well," Christian said confidently, hoping he wasn't being taken for a complete fool. He had no idea if that was a good wage or not.

Soon he was done up in green-and-white livery with gold braid and buttons. He thought he looked like a leprechaun, and he felt about the same way he had in the blue velvet suit, but Mrs. Clover was enthusiastic.

"Well, don't you look a proper sight," she said. "Put a crown and some ermine on you and I could pass you off as a suitor for Princess Marigold. Oh, my goodness, that reminds me. We've got to get busy. There's a state dinner brewing tonight for Princess Marigold's suitors, Prince Cyprian of Upper Lower Grevania, and Sir Magnus of . . . well, of nowhere. Jeremy broke his arm, falling down the back staircase with King Swithbert's breakfast tray this morning, so you'll be serving. I'm turning you over to Sedgewick, the head butler, for training. You'd better be a quick study because we haven't much time."

Christian *was* a quick study. In fact, the instructions were so simple and straightforward, he could only figure that anyone who couldn't get them would be, as Ed would say, dumb as a box of doornails.

Sedgewick was in quite a twitter, as was apparently everyone in the castle, because of the evening's dinner for Prince Cyprian and Sir Magnus, the shirt-tail relative. Well, Magnus had some minor title— Baronet of something-or-other—but it was only a courtesy title, without any property or wealth. So he was by far the more motivated suitor, according to Sedgewick. He wanted a kingdom at least as much as he wanted a princess. The servants, in general, favored Prince Cyprian. He seemed more relaxed.

"But he would be, wouldn't he?" Christian observed. "Because he's not trying as hard. Sir Magnus has more at stake and therefore more to lose." Christian knew from hunting that the harder one tried, the more likely one was to make some perfectly stupid mistake that blew the whole operation.

"Indeed, yes," Sedgewick answered, giving Christian an appraising look. This was no ordinary serving boy, he could see that. Not at all.

As time neared for the state dinner, the atmosphere behind the scenes became ever more tense. It was a relief when the trumpets finally sounded, announcing the procession into the dining hall. At last the action could begin.

6

Christian had to admit he was dying for a look at these suitors. He wondered if either of them had ever read any Greek myths. Or watched the stars, or taught tricks to dogs; if either of them had any idea of what it took to be a best friend. His station was at the wine table, and his job was to keep the glasses filled. He reviewed the order of wines as he stood at his station, waiting for the diners to make their stately way in.

King Swithbert came first, with Queen Olympia, shimmering in damask and diamonds, holding his arm. He looked even older than he had through the telescope, and the queen's grip on him seemed more supportive than affectionate. She, on the other hand, was beautifully maintained and even quite radiant, a look perhaps achieved by artificial means. Under the arm not supporting the king, she carried Fenleigh, his eyes narrow and glittering. The animal wore a gold collar and chain leash.

"She never goes anywhere without that ferret," Sedgewick whispered to Christian. "Talks to him like she expects him to answer back. Even asks his advice about things."

The king and queen were followed by various courtiers and relatives and hangers-on. Prince Cyprian entered alone, clad in white and gold, his blond ringlets adorned with a crown of topaz and pearls. He looked quite pleased with himself. Behind him, also alone, came Sir Magnus. He could hardly have been more of a contrast to Prince Cyprian. He was tall, dark, and handsome in his black-and-silver finery, walking as if he owned the world. Only his quick blink and the worried pucker between his eyebrows gave away the fact that he knew he didn't—not even a little piece of it.

Last of all, almost an afterthought at her own party, came Princess Marigold, trailed by her three little dogs. Christian had to steady himself against the wine table, and his heart was beating so hard he was sure she would be able to hear it. The expression on her face made it plain to anyone who looked at her—and hardly anyone did, Christian observed—that she wished she were anywhere but where she was. He could see the corner of a book protruding from the pocket of her Prussian blue gown, which gave it a homey, personal look in spite of the ruffles, furbelows, poufs, bows, and brilliants that somebody, completely misunderstanding her style, had got her up in. The crown she wore was too much as well. Too big, too heavy, too gaudy. She looked like somebody forced to go to a costume party and not enjoying it a whit. But to be so close to her after seeing her only through a telescope for so long—why, what did Hayes mean, saying she was plain? Her skin was clear, her eyes were bright and curious, her hair was shining—well, she was beautiful, that's all. His beautiful, unreachable princess.

Marigold sat herself at the foot of the table, her chin in one hand. The little dogs trampled around on her puddled skirts for a while until the diners, freely imbibing of Christian's rapid pourings, began to drop morsels of their dinners onto the floor. Then the dogs took to grazing under the table, vacuuming up anything that fell. Christian couldn't help thinking how much Bub and Cate would have enjoyed such an opportunity. And thanks to Ed's etiquette book, he knew that dropped tidbits were supposed to be left for the dogs.

Prince Cyprian deliberately slipped pieces of roasted meats beneath the table, making sure Marigold saw him do it, and then watched as the little dogs gobbled them up. It was hard for Christian not to be partial to a dog lover even when he didn't want to like either of Marigold's suitors. He watched Sir Magnus to see if he would take any special interest in the dogs. Magnus never even looked at them—or at Marigold, either, for that matter. He concentrated only on the array of silverware on either side of his plate, uncertainly picking up first one fork and then another, with a perplexed frown. Christian could have told him that the oyster fork was the small one with the three tines.

Sir Magnus didn't drop any meat on purpose—in fact, he hardly ate at all. Christian could see his knees jiggling nervously under the table. This was definitely a fellow out of his depth and sure to be trying too hard. And Chris knew what could happen under those circumstances.

Christian was the only one to notice when Prince Cyprian deliberately dropped a piece of meat onto the toe of Sir Magnus's shoe. So it didn't surprise Chris in the slightest when one of Marigold's dogs sank his teeth into Sir Magnus's elegant instep. Startled, Magnus jerked reflexively out of his chair and kicked the little creature halfway across the dining hall.

Marigold screamed and jumped to her feet.

"Oh, well done!" one of the courtiers shouted to Magnus. "Though hardly sporting."

Instinctively, Christian rushed to the dog and picked it up a split second before Princess Marigold reached it. Breathless at being so close to her, Christian handed the yelping dog to the princess without a word. Their hands touched beneath the furry body, and then their eyes met.

Christian felt as if he'd downed a fast couple of glasses of the Château Mutton de Rothschild '47 that he'd just been pouring for the banquet guests.

"Oh my," Princess Marigold whispered. Then, cradling the whimpering dog, she turned and called, "Flopsy! Mopsy!" The remaining two dogs ran to her, and together, the little retinue swept out of the dining room.

Queen Olympia rose from her seat. "Marigold!" she shouted. "You come back here!" Fenleigh raised his head and bared his teeth, approximating Olympia's look.

Marigold, her back straight and stiff, kept going. She attempted to slam the tall dining hall doors behind her, but two burly footmen caught them before they could crash shut. Marigold hurried on, rushing up the sweeping staircase with her dogs.

Christian had to admire the arm on her, shoving those heavy doors so hard while holding on to her distressed pet.

"What?" King Swithbert said. "What happened to Marigold?" Nobody paid any attention to him.

"I say, old chap," Prince Cyprian said smugly to Sir Magnus, "do you think that furthered your suit with the princess?"

"It was an accident," Sir Magnus muttered unhappily. "The little devil scared me. I never liked dogs, anyway."

"Well, it's done now," Prince Cyprian gloated. "Accident or not, I wonder what you can do to atone. I'm quite sure she took note of the way I generously fed the little . . . devils, as you so colorfully call them. Did you know she raised them after their mother died? Fed them with a baby bottle every four hours around the clock, I'm told. She couldn't love them more if they were her own children."

"I didn't know that," Sir Magnus said, stricken. Then he straightened his shoulders and affected a more manly demeanor, though Christian could see that his knees were shaking under the table. "I'm sure I'll be able to explain to the princess what happened."

Christian no longer favored the smug and crafty Prince Cyprian. But he wasn't so much in favor of Magnus, either, who seemed harmless enough but not even close to Marigold in spirit, brains, and grit. To be honest, he didn't like thinking about Marigold marrying *anybody*. It gave him a pang right in the center of his chest.

Marigold never came back to the table, even though Queen Olympia sent several volleys of servants to fetch her. King Swithbert kept asking what was going on, but nobody ever answered him. Cyprian and Magnus gave each other suspicious glances for the rest of the dinner, and the other guests got so rowdy that by the time the dessert arrived, there had been five fights, three threatened duels, and one broken engagement. Christian wondered whether five kinds of wine at dinner was really such a good idea. And he wondered where Marigold had gone and what she was doing. He bet she could use a best friend right about now.

It was very late when the dinner was over, the entertainers had finished their juggling and dancing and madrigal singing, and the guests had staggered off to their beds.

Christian and the other servants were left to tidy up the mess that had been made of the dining hall—spilled wine, scattered nutshells, dropped utensils, and various forgotten handkerchiefs, veils, shawls, and, inexplicably, a set of wooden false teeth. Christian knew that if these people had to pick up after themselves for just one week, they'd learn to be a lot tidier. Even he had learned to clean up the messes he made with his inventions. Being waited on hand and foot was not good for one's personal development.

When he finally made it to his sleeping place in the straw of the stable loft, he was so exhausted, physically and emotionally, that he was out like a log, as Ed would have said. His last thought as he plunged into sleep was of his hand touching Marigold's under the distressed dog—and remembering that with that touch, she could tell his thoughts.

EDRIC SLEPT hardly at all. Bub and Cate were unsettled, too. The only thing on all their minds was, Where was Christian? There was no way to be sure he'd made it to the castle. Or, if he had, that there was a job waiting for him. And if there wasn't, would he come home or would he move on, trying to prove himself? Ed felt awful. What had he been thinking, urging Chris to go away?

Sometimes things that seem like good ideas in theory, in practice turn out to be the worst kinds of boneheaded blunders.

Ed flopped and turned, and shoved the dogs—
huddling near him for reassurance—this way and
that. Finally, near dawn, he drifted off, figuring that
there was nothing he could do about it now; it was all
spilled milk over the dam.

7

The next morning Christian was in the scullery repairing a butter churn. As he worked on it, he got an idea for a more efficient way to operate the dasher. He needed a chain and a handle and a gear, that's all. Thinking about such things was easier than thinking about Marigold, who had never seemed so far away.

Mrs. Clover, swamped with the demands of the extra guests at the castle, shooed him off to the blacksmith's, where he found what he needed in a pile of discarded parts at the back of the shop.

"Handy, are you?" the smith asked. He was a burly man, red-faced from the heat of his forge, wearing a leather apron.

"I like to build things," Christian said. "It's fun."

"Me, too. You should see some of the things I've made. Great stuff. But not everything works out, does it? Not my perpetual-motion machine, or my flying machine, or my corn picker. You might be interested in having a look at my failures. They're dumped in the dungeon. Maybe there'd be some parts you could use."

"The dungeon?"

"Oh, it hasn't been used as a *dungeon* dungeon since old King Swithbert took the throne. He's too softhearted to torture anybody. He prefers to exile troublemakers. Queen Olympia, she's another story. If she were ruler, that dungeon would have standing room only. That's why I'm rooting for Sir Magnus to marry the princess. Then Marigold'll get to be queen when poor old King Swithbert croaks."

Chris got that pang in his chest again. "I served at the state dinner last night. She doesn't seem very interested in either one of her suitors."

"She may not be, but I think the queen sure is. She's ready to have a wedding. She's been running candidates through here for a year, and the princess has turned up her nose at all of them. And when Olympia runs out of patience—look out."

This was not good news to Christian. "Well, thanks for the stuff," he said. "If it works the way I think it will, pretty soon butter making's going to be a lot faster around here."

"Let me know how it turns out." The blacksmith brought his hammer down on the soup ladle he was fashioning on the anvil. A great shower of sparks exploded outward like fireworks as Christian headed back to the kitchen.

Meg, the scullery maid, was overjoyed at the new butter churn. "Oh, look how fast it goes," she said, turning the handle. "There'll be butter in no time, without me breaking me arms hauling that dasher up and down. Oh, Christian, luv, you've made a miracle, you have. And I'll not be forgetting it." She looked up at him from under her eyelashes. "Maybe I can find a way to thank you."

Christian, ignorant of the art of flirting, said, "Don't worry about it. I enjoyed fixing it."

"Well, I'd enjoy thanking you, I know I would," she said, batting her lashes and turning the churn handle in a way that displayed her shapely figure to advantage.

Christian, uncomfortable, shrugged. "Well. You're welcome."

The next chore Sedgewick assigned Christian was to begin repairs on a section of the wall bordering the terrace overlooking the river.

"And if the princess is out on the terrace, and she is out there a lot," Sedgewick said, "whatever you do, don't touch her."

"I wouldn't think of it," Christian said obediently, though there was hardly anything he'd like more. "I know she's a princess and I'm just a servant." That was perfectly true, but—though he knew better—it was something he kept hoping didn't really matter.

"Well, I couldn't help noticing how you picked up that little dog last night—Poopsy or Nutsy or whatever its name is. I can never keep them straight. Did your hand happen to touch hers when you handed the dog back?"

"Oh no," Christian lied through his teeth. Her hand had felt wonderful—soft and strong at the same time.

"Good. Because if she touches you, she can tell what you're thinking."

When Marigold had first told him about her curse, Christian had had to ponder for a minute before he realized how bad that could be. At first all he thought was: What a lot of junk mail she must receive from other people's minds. But then he realized why people feared her—all their mean and hateful thoughts, the ones best kept to themselves, would be exposed.

He knew exactly what he had been thinking when their hands touched. Some concerns about the dog, and some uncharitable thoughts about her suitors, but mostly how happy he was to be so close to her. Not until this very moment did he consider how offensive she might have found that—a servant feeling that way about her. No wonder she'd said "Oh my," and run away.

Sedgewick went on. "Only King Swithbert doesn't mind touching her. But his head seems to be filled with nothing but harmless, woolly thoughts wishing ill upon no one. The others in the palace, I'm afraid, are not so willing to have their thoughts inspected. Well, get to work," Sedgewick said, giving Christian a basket full of the tools he'd need. "And don't forget— no touching."

The terrace wall was in worse shape than Christian expected—much worse than it had looked from the other side, through the telescope. The mortar between the stones was crumbling to powder and would have to be completely replaced before someone leaned on the wall and it collapsed, dumping them into the river below. This was a big job. He rolled up his sleeves and set to work.

He was concentrating so hard, he didn't hear when Princess Marigold came out onto the terrace and sat down to read. Not until her little floor-mop dogs began barking as they played did he turn and notice.

He stood up to stretch out his back and then doffed his cap to her. On the other side of the river, a friendship with her had seemed completely natural. But here, where everyone's rank was the first thing you had to think about, he wondered how he had ever been innocent enough, or stupid enough, to think that she'd want a mere servant for her best friend, no matter how lonely she was. He felt sad and foolish.

"Good morning," she said. "You're the one who picked up Topsy last night, aren't you?"

"Yes, Your Highness," Christian answered cautiously. Was it possible she'd been too distracted to remember his thoughts? "Is she all right?"

"As you can see," Princess Marigold said, pointing to where the three little dogs frolicked. "But I was worried at first. Thank you for coming to her rescue."

"Don't mention it," he said. "I have—uh, *had*—dogs of my own, back home. I know how attached you get."

"What kind of dogs?" she asked, putting down her book.

That was his Marigold—always curious. "Oh . . . a big one and a small one," he said evasively, realizing it would not be wise to describe dogs she'd be sure to recognize from his p-mail. "Mutts, I guess you'd say. Your Highness," he added quickly.

"You must miss them," she said. "Who takes care of them now?"

"My—" Christian stopped. He couldn't say his foster father. That's the way he'd described Ed to her. Princess Marigold was watching him, expectant, her head tipped slightly to one side.

"My friend Edric," Christian finally said. But he wished he could touch Marigold now so that she could see into his mind and know, without the woeful inadequacy of words, all that Ed—whom he was missing painfully just then—was and had been to him.

ACROSS THE RIVER, Ed stood on the ledge above the waterfall, the telescope trained on the riverfront terrace. In his desperation to know what had happened to Christian, he had decided to look for him.

Imagine his surprise when he saw Christian, splendid in his green-and-white livery with the gold braid and buttons—protected by an apron embroidered with the royal coat of arms—standing casually by the parapet, talking to the princess!

Well, blow me over with a feather! Ed thought. He'd known Christian's correspondence with her was risky, but he'd thought Chris would at least have the sense to remain anonymous once he got over there. She was a *princess*, for pete's sake, and he was just a commoner—though he was so extraordinary and talented and so special to Ed that he really couldn't consider him common in any way. But the princess would. And Ed could only think she'd be embarrassed and offended to know her p-mail pal was a lowly servant—who then had the nerve and the poor judgment to confess who he was. Why, Christian could end up in the dungeon, screwed to the rack, or locked into the iron maiden. Or worse, far worse, introduced to Madame Guillotine.

Ed looked sadly down at the dogs at his feet. "I guess that's the last we'll be seeing of him, guys. I should have been a better parent." Bub and Cate whined in commiseration. Ed lowered the telescope and tramped off into the forest. Maybe he'd find something out there today that would cheer him up, though he couldn't possibly imagine what that might be.

IT DEFINITELY wasn't Queen Mab, whom he came across sitting on a stump. Her wee reading glasses were perched on the end of her nose as she puzzled over a scrawled map that even Ed could see was completely incomprehensible.

"You'll never get where you're going with that thing," he said.

"Oh, what do you know?" she retorted.

"I know enough to know that map's a mess."

"I'll have you know my mapmaker is the best there is." Queen Mab turned the map around and looked at it with the other side up.

"Who says?"

"Well, he does, of course," she said, scratching her head with one of the pencils stuck in her hair.

"He's probably the only one," Ed muttered. "Why don't you admit you need some competent help?"

"Meaning you, I suppose?" she scoffed.

"How overdue are you picking up that batch of teeth?" he asked, indicating the long list of names on the stump next to her.

She snatched up the list. "None of your business."

"That's what I thought," he said. "Sooner or later, Mab, you're going to have some competition from me. Count on it."

"You're going to need a lot more support for that to happen," she said, folding the map.

"And I'll get it," he said, not at all sure that he would. "Arrogance and inflexibility aren't good for any business, you know. A closed mind gathers no moss."

"Whatever that means," Mab said, flying off.

Ed watched her weave uncertainly through the trees, and then trudged home feeling even worse than he had when he'd set out.

8

I don't remember seeing you before," the princess said to Christian. "Although somehow you seem familiar. Have we met?"

How he wished he could answer that question. "I've only been working here since yesterday. I was lucky that more servants were needed because of the festivities for Prince Cyprian and Sir Magnus."

"I'm glad you got a job," Marigold said, "but I wish there weren't so many festivities." She sighed gustily and flopped back in her chair.

"You like a quieter life?" he asked politely, knowing full well that she'd like a life with equal parts adventure and hominess.

"Well, not entirely. Just one without so many suitors in it."

"Just one suitor, perhaps?" Christian suggested.

"Only if he were the right one," she said a bit wistfully. "And I think the one I want is one I'll never have."

"Oh?" he said. He felt as if his ears had perked up the way Cate's did when she heard something interesting. "How can you be so sure?"

"It's simple. If I can't meet him, I can't have him."

"But can't a princess meet anybody she wants to meet?"

"Not if he lives far away. And is a commoner to boot."

Christian's cheeks grew hot. "It sounds as if you've got someone specific in mind."

She gave him a sharp look, reminding him that he was, after all, in the presence of royalty. "Never mind," she said. "But just tell me one thing. Do you think it's necessary for a woman to marry?"

Christian's brow furrowed. Well, he was definitely the wrong person to answer that question. He knew totally zip about what went on between men and women as far as marriage was concerned. "I suppose not," he said slowly while he thought fast. "Unless there was something she wanted that she could get only by being married."

She stood up so suddenly that the book in her lap hit the flagstones. "Exactly!" she said. "That's what I must tell my parents. There's nothing I want badly enough to marry one of those...those...well, those suitors...to get it."

He knew he should probably keep his mouth shut, but he wanted to make sure she'd thought of everything. He didn't want her realizing later that she'd overlooked something and blame him for giving her bad advice. Who knew how a princess's blame might express itself? The rack? The iron maiden? Maybe even...the guillotine? "What about...I mean, have you thought of children?"

She regarded him gravely. "Yes," she said slowly. "And even though everybody says they're a lot of trouble, and messy and demanding, I still want them. I can be a lot of trouble and messy and demanding, too, so I know how that is."

So can I! Christian wanted to add.

"What I like best about them is they're so accepting and nonjudgmental."

Chris made a dubious sound.

"What?"

"I'm not sure I agree with you about that. I was pretty judgmental as a little kid." At least until he'd come to live with Ed, he remembered. After that, he'd liked just about everything.

"Well, if I get a child like you, I think I can handle it," she said.

Was she insulting him? Dismissing him? He felt as if he'd been slapped.

"Anyway, if I don't get married, I can always adopt some children," Marigold went on. "It seems like people are forever dying to get rid of them—leaving them on church doorsteps, or out in the forest, or in baskets on the river. There's never a shortage of unwanted children."

"But the succession—can an adopted child inherit the throne?"

"Why not? It would be my child, the child of my heart, and if I were queen, it would be my successor." She waved a hand. "If there's a problem with that, one of my sisters' children can inherit. They already have more than they need to take care of the successions in their own kingdoms. Who knows if a child of mine would be suited to rule, anyway? Not everybody is."

"It would be," Christian said emphatically. "With you for its mother, it would have all the right qualities."

She was bending to pick up her book, then stopped

halfway down and looked at him. *Really* looked at him. "What an odd thing to say," she said. "My mother doesn't believe I can do anything right. She says I'm too democratic."

"Your mother's wrong," he said, gazing ardently into her eyes—and wondering when she would decide he was way too insolent for a servant and have the dungeon cleaned out for him.

But instead she rushed over to him and grabbed his hands in hers. Her eyes looked off over his shoulder, focusing on something that seemed inside herself. "Oh!" she cried and let go, then ran away from him to gather her book and her dogs. Just as she was dashing to the stone archway leading indoors, her parents came sweeping out, followed by Prince Cyprian, Sir Magnus, a gaggle of courtiers and hangers-on, and servants carrying folding chairs, parasols, rugs, and trays of food.

"Ah, Marigold," said King Swithbert. "So happy we've found you. We're having a lovely luncheon alfresco today and have been looking for you to join us."

"I'm afraid I can't," she said. "I seem to have developed a sick headache."

Christian couldn't be sure, but he thought she'd flashed him a glance. Was she thinking, as he was, of Bub and *his* sick headaches, the ones he got from pretending to be brave? Had she discerned who he was from holding his hands? If she had, why had it distressed her so? And why had she grabbed his hands in the first place? Wasn't that an unusual way for a princess to behave with a servant?

"A little fresh air will be just the thing, then," Queen Olympia said, herding Marigold away from the archway without actually touching her.

"Yes," Prince Cyprian said languidly. "It won't be a party without you."

"I wish you would stay," Sir Magnus said, awkwardly taking her hand—the one holding the book—and kissing it with a loud smacking sound. Everyone but King Swithbert took an involuntary step backward.

Christian was surprised to see that Magnus wasn't afraid to touch Marigold. Maybe he was thinking only complimentary thoughts. Or maybe the book in Marigold's hand somehow interfered with her ability to perceive his thoughts. Or maybe, as Christian suspected, Magnus's head was so empty, there were too few thoughts to read.

"We missed you at dinner last night," Cyprian said, stifling a yawn. "The party wasn't the same without you."

"Indeed not," King Swithbert chimed in. "Much less . . . or perhaps much more . . . well, you know how it is."

Christian imagined that the contents of King Swithbert's head must look like the junk pile in the blacksmith shop.

"You there," one of the other servants called to Christian. "Come help us lay out this luncheon."

Obediently, Chris unrolled carpets and carried tables and set up chairs while the guests stood around waiting impatiently for their picnic to be presented to them. Then he packed up his tools for the unfinished job on the wall, so as not to offend the royalty with signs of honest, sweaty, satisfying labor.

He was in the kitchen eating bread and cheese for lunch when Meg, the scullery maid, came in with a trayful of dirty dishes. "I swear, these royal people are useless," she said. "All they ever do is eat and change their clothes—especially the queen. That woman must wear six outfits a day. Sure, they wouldn't know an honest day's work if it bit them in the—" She stopped and giggled.

"They've never had to work," Christian said, "so they can't know the satisfaction of a job well done. Still, they don't seem to do any harm."

"No need to worry about harm around here," she retorted. "This kingdom has been peaceful since I was a baby. The king does nothing for us."

"Perhaps the kingdom has been peaceful for so long because of the way the king has ruled."

Meg made a face. "Oh, never mind that. I'm just ever so grateful for that new butter churn you fashioned. The butter makes so much faster now."

"I'm glad you like it. I enjoy inventing things."

She came up next to him, where he sat over his bread and cheese in the quiet kitchen, and put her arms around him. "It's just about the nicest thing anybody's ever done for me!" she exclaimed.

"Well, I didn't do it just for...," Christian began, but before he could finish, she kissed him full on the mouth.

Well, here was something the etiquette book had never covered. What *was* the proper response to this situation? Would it be rude if he pushed her away? Was it necessary to kiss her back?

Before he could decide what to do, there was the thud of boots on the kitchen's stone floor followed by a strangled roar and the unmistakable metallic ring of a sword being unsheathed. At that, Meg sprang back from Christian, and the two of them looked up into the furious countenance of Rollo, the guard from the drawbridge.

"Meg!" he bellowed, drawn up to his full height of eight feet, two inches. "You said you were finished with this sort of thing!"

"'Twasn't me," she said, backing away from Christian and pointing. "'Twas him."

"No, I didn't—" Christian stopped short, the point of the sword an inch from his nose.

"Oh, don't, Rollo," Meg cried, throwing her arms around as much of the giant as she could reach. "He meant no harm. You always say I'm the prettiest wench in the castle, don't you, now? Can I help it if I draw men to me like flies to honey?"

The sword point moved back an inch.

She went on. "Can you really blame him?" She tightened her embrace, and her voice took on an even more cajoling tone. "It only proves what excellent taste you have." When the sword point stayed where it was, she added, "You should save your sword arm"— she scrambled up onto a chair to stroke his biceps— "for other uses."

Gradually Rollo lowered the sword, and Christian began to breathe again. He wanted to explain what had happened but decided that perhaps keeping his mouth shut just now would be the smarter thing. Rollo wouldn't believe him anyway, no matter what he said.

"One more time," Rollo said, waving the sword in front of Christian. "If I have just one more problem with you, no one in the kingdom will be able to save you. Am I clear?"

Christian simply stared back. It took a terrific amount of effort not to look away, but Rollo needed to know he wasn't dealing with some chickenhearted invertebrate.

Then the sword waggled toward the door. "Now get out of here."

Christian resisted the impulse to hurry. He gave Rollo one last long look and then turned, picked up his bread and cheese, and left the kitchen. He'd eat outside.

9

Sedgewick was polishing a great silver samovar in the summer pantry when Christian came in. He'd puzzled long and hard, over his bread and cheese, about what had happened with Meg and Rollo—and he was puzzling still.

"What's with the frown?" Sedgewick asked. "Anybody would think Rollo caught you kissing Meg."

"How did you know?" Christian asked, astounded. Did Sedgewick have the same curse as Princess Marigold, without the need for touching?

Sedgewick's eyebrows shot up. "You were? He did?" He put his hand over his eyes. "I should have warned you, but I never thought she'd act so fast.

She's Rollo's girl, and Rollo has the worst temper of anybody in the kingdom, except maybe Queen Olympia. But Meg has an eye for the lads, and Rollo knows it, so he keeps a close watch on her. And anybody who messes with her goes on his blacklist forever. That's why she picks on the new lads. Everybody else knows better. Unless they're trying to commit suicide."

"But I didn't do the kissing," Christian said. "It was her. She started it."

"Meg's a friendly girl, no doubt about it," Sedgewick said. "Exactly the kind of girl you want to watch your step with." And then he explained a few essential facts to Christian about women and manners and being smart about both. "Now, I think you'd better get back to work on that wall. The queen wants it done in time for the wedding she's determined to have."

As Christian lugged his basket of tools back up to the riverside terrace, he felt like a complete bumpkin and a total fool to boot. The smart thing would have been to have stayed in the cave with Ed, where he understood his life and couldn't get into any trouble. But the urge to see more of the world had been too strong—and was still strong, in spite of Meg and Rollo and the pain of having Marigold so close yet so unreachable. He felt alive in a way he hadn't known was possible on the other side of the river. And strangely, that sense he'd always had of something big coming, of some...some *purpose* awaiting him, was more powerful than ever.

The big lesson he'd learned today was that the etiquette book didn't solve every problem. There were some situations where he'd have to rely on his own common sense—which he was quickly, out of necessity, acquiring more of.

And he knew that he and Rollo would be having another confrontation.

As he came around a turn in the stone staircase that led up to the terrace, he heard a woman speaking and stopped. Someone must have left open the door to a room in the hallway off the staircase. He hadn't expected to be faced with another manners dilemma so soon. What was the proper etiquette for a situation like *this*? The speaker apparently wasn't aware that she could be overheard. Should he make a noise to let her know he was coming? Or tiptoe silently away? Or keep going as if he were deaf? Or perhaps gently shut the door?

As he stood wondering, he couldn't help overhearing every word she was saying.

"Ah, Fenleigh, which one do you think Marigold should marry? Cyprian, so she can go off to Upper

Lower Grevania? Or Magnus, so she can stay here and keep me from being queen?"

Christian heard a faint growl.

"Oh yes," Olympia said. "I think so, too. Better for her to be far away. If she stays here with Magnus—well, there's no telling what sort of accident she might need to have, is there? Maybe one that involved poor old Swithbert, too. Wouldn't that be a shame, Fenleigh? My husband and daughter gone in one stroke."

Again Chris heard the growl. And once he'd heard Marigold's name and the threat associated with it, he knew he wasn't going to be doing any tiptoeing away.

"Oh, I know she doesn't love Magnus or Cyprian—she doesn't even *like* them—but what does that have to do with anything? Royal marriages aren't made for love—surely you don't think I married Swithbert for love, do you, Fenleigh? Royal marriages are made out of necessity—for alliances, for trade, and for heirs."

There was a silence interrupted by the clink of glass against glass, and the sound of lapping. "There, Fenleigh, did a nice drinkie make you feel better? You know, since Magnus has no realm of his own, think how grateful he'd be, as a bereaved widower, if I set him up with a little manor house somewhere and a small fiefdom he couldn't get into too much mischief with. He wouldn't make any trouble for me." Her voice hardened. "Not if he's sensible, he wouldn't."

Again the growl.

"Well, Marigold needs to choose. Enough reading, and playing with those awful dogs that chase you around all the time, and fussing with her plants. It's time for her to become more . . . more regal. And the farther away the better. But if she's close . . . well, that can be managed, too. After all, I do look quite well in black. Don't you agree, Fenleigh?"

Christian gasped and then clapped a hand over his mouth. Picking her nose and wiping her hands on her dogs wouldn't work for Marigold this time. Olympia sounded determined. And if Marigold did manage to scare Cyprian off, Magnus would be harder to discourage. He needed a place to live even more than he needed a bride.

Christian had to get out of there before he got caught listening, and go someplace where he could think. Hastily, he turned and tiptoed down the stairs as fast as he could go.

"Did you hear something, Fenleigh?" Queen Olympia asked, as Christian made it around the next bend in the stairs.

Chris heard the click of heels coming down the

stairs behind him, and he went faster, the sound of his footsteps masked by the clicking and the growling. At the landing, he ducked into an alcove covered by a heavy velvet curtain. He stood in the dark behind the curtain, holding his basket of tools against his chest like a shield. He could feel things around him, but he could see nothing.

The heels went across the landing and on down the stairs, and Christian let out the breath he'd been holding for so long he was almost blue. But he stayed where he was. What if Queen Olympia came silently up the stairs again and caught him cowering there like the guilty eavesdropper he was?

After waiting what seemed a week, he carefully pulled the heavy curtain aside an inch and peered out. The landing and the stairs, for as far as he could see, were empty. The light that then came into the alcove showed him he was surrounded by suits of armor. If he'd made even a slight move in the wrong direction, many pounds of metallic figures would have fallen over in a cataract of noise that would have sealed his fate in an instant. Then he would have wished that Rollo's sword had put a swift end to him in the kitchen.

His heart thumping, Christian stepped out from behind the curtain, holding his basket carefully so the tools wouldn't clank together. He stood for a moment, listening. He heard nothing. Then, in spite of his already galloping heartbeat, he tore up the stairs as if a pack of rabid dogs were at his heels.

He was surprised to find the luncheon party still lolling about on the terrace, sipping their wine and sponging happily off the generous and dotty King Swithbert. The king seemed so pleased to be surrounded by his relatives and guests, and was apparently unaware that at least some of them were there not from affection or for the pleasure of his company but for the free meals and lavish entertainment.

Christian wondered if he had really just heard Queen Olympia suggesting a convenient accident for both Marigold and King Swithbert if Marigold married Magnus. Convenient for the queen, that is—certainly not for Swithbert and Marigold.

Oh, he needed Ed now more than he had in his entire life. Whom else could he talk to about what he'd overheard? Whom else could he trust? No matter how much he might be learning to trust himself, it was still good to have another person to double-check things with.

Was this how Ed had meant for him to learn to be independent? By having things like this happen to him and by then having to manage them by himself?

He felt as if he'd lived a whole lifetime of emotions

in the two days that he'd been at the castle. The existence he'd lived with Ed seemed as far away as a fairy tale—one he didn't know if he could fit back into.

As fraught as his current situation was, he felt wide awake and alert in a way he never had before. Now he needed to use all his brains and skills and courage to find out if King Swithbert and Marigold were really in any danger, or if Queen Olympia had just been musing to herself—and to Fenleigh. He was pretty sure this wasn't a situation that was covered in the etiquette book.

He lingered in the archway at the top of the staircase, wondering if it would be all right for him to begin work again while the royal party was still there.

Princess Marigold stood apart from the others, tossing a ball for her dogs to chase. Prince Cyprian sat in a chair nearby, applauding when one of the dogs made a successful catch.

"Bravo!" he called. "So clever! So athletic! So well-trained. By such a—" He paused. "An accomplished mistress," he finished.

Christian snorted from the shadows under the archway. Some suitor he was. Why didn't he call her lovely, or enchanting, or fascinating? *Accomplished?* That was like complimenting someone on their spelling or their dish-washing abilities. Barely praise at all. Why, if he were her suitor, he'd have plenty of things he could say. Wasn't Cyprian paying any attention at all to what she was like? Couldn't he see how curious she was, how loving to her dogs and her befuddled father, how capable in running her perfume business, how loyal, how bright, and how spirited? And how lonely she must be, surrounded by people who wanted only to use her for their own ends and who wouldn't even touch her for fear of revealing that?

Christian had a feeling she knew it without having to touch anyone.

He was becoming more hot under the collar by the moment. He had to calm himself down. Because even if he could tell these things to Prince Cyprian, what good would it do? Inexperienced as he was, he knew that you couldn't talk someone into loving somebody. Loving had to happen on its own.

King Swithbert spotted Chris lingering in the archway. "Come, come, young man," he beckoned. "If you're here to work, you should get to it. Don't mind us. We won't interfere."

Several of the courtiers snickered. As if they would *dream* of involving themselves with actual useful labor. Swithbert, dotty as he was supposed to be, at least seemed to understand that work had to be done, sometimes at an inconvenient moment.

Christian carried his tools to the wall and began scraping out the old crumbling mortar as quietly as he could, trying to remain inconspicuous. Far across the river, he could see the waterfall where once he'd bathed, and from where he'd watched this very terrace on which he never expected to be standing.

He heard Princess Marigold ask Prince Cyprian, "Have you ever read the Greek myths?"

"Greek myths, Greek myths," he repeated. "Can't say that I have. I'm not much of a reader. Why do you ask? Do I remind you of any of the gods?"

"I was thinking of Narcissus. He was so handsome that every woman he met fell in love with him."

"How kind of you." Prince Cyprian preened. "How very kind."

Christian ducked his head to hide a smile. Narcissus was handsome, all right, but the only person he loved was himself. He sat by a pool staring at his own reflection in the water for so long that he forgot to eat and drink, and so he wasted away to his death.

Princess Marigold caught Christian's eye, and he realized she'd seen his smile. He hoped he wasn't going to be punished. Perhaps she had meant to give

Cyprian an honest compliment. But no. The way she gave him a faint smile in return made them conspirators. How clever she was. How subtle and smart. Prince Cyprian wasn't good enough to carry her train. What a choice her mother was going to insist she make, Christian thought: Cyprian or Magnus.

If only there were a way for him to give her a third choice.

10

As Christian worked on the wall, Prince Cyprian rose from his chair and approached King Swithbert, drawing him apart from the rest of the party, closer to Christian. Like all servants, Chris was invisible to those he served—at least until they wanted something from him or he did something wrong.

"Listen, Swithbert, old man," Cyprian said. "You know this daughter of yours is a hard sell in the marriage market. I mean, the fact of her curse, and that she's plainer than those bombshell sisters of hers. And smart. Don't forget about that. Not many men wanting to take on a smart woman these days, you know."

"She *is* smart, isn't she?" King Swithbert agreed, sounding proud. "And pretty nice, too, don't you think?" He beamed benevolently at Prince Cyprian.

"Oh sure, of course, nice as pie," Cyprian said quickly. "But a hard sell all the same. You may not know this, but I've also been approached by the kingdoms of Skydonia, Figland, and Sproon to court their princesses, all of whom are prettier and more charming than your Geranium."

"Marigold." King Swithbert sounded irritated.

"Right. Marigold. So, what do you think about sweetening the pot a little?"

"Sweetening the pot?" the king asked.

"You know, beefing up the dowry. To get somebody to take her off your hands."

"Why, I'm not looking for someone to take her off my hands," King Swithbert said, blinking up at Prince Cyprian, who, Christian had to admit, was pretty dazzling with the sunlight bouncing off his golden curls and gilded crown. "I'm looking for someone for her to be happy with, a companion and best friend for a lifetime. The dowry is to make sure she'll have what she needs when I'm no longer the one taking care of her. It's not a bribe."

Prince Cyprian drummed his fingertips on the wall. "No. Of course not. Not a bribe at all. But you do want to make sure she's well taken care of, don't you?"

"Certainly I do. I've been to Upper Lower Grevania, young man. I know it's a wealthy kingdom. And I know you could provide quite adequately for her even without *any* dowry. What are you trying to do here?"

So King Swithbert wasn't the dim bulb he might appear, Christian mused. At least not when it came to Marigold.

Prince Cyprian took a step back and drew himself up to his full height. "I don't like what you're suggesting," he said pompously, annoyed at being so accurately appraised. "You must know I have nothing but the greatest regard for you and all your family. But I am in great demand as a suitor, and I only want to make sure that I get the best arrangement for myself that I can. And for my future queen, too," he put in as an afterthought. "Under these gravely insulting circumstances, I shall have to withdraw my offer for your daughter's hand. My retinue and I will be leaving for Upper Lower Grevania as soon as we can get our bags packed. Which should be in the morning. After breakfast."

"Fine with me," King Swithbert said, and returned to the table where he'd been playing a game of snip-snapsnorum with his chancellor of the exchequer.

Prince Cyprian gathered his entourage, and they clattered off down the stairs, in huffs and dudgeons, even though most of them didn't know what was going on. The rest of the guests, including Magnus, fearing that they had missed an announcement about the next event, hastened after them.

It was a sure thing now that Marigold would be married off to Magnus, a man who might be decent enough but who didn't love her, couldn't possibly appreciate her, and only wanted a secure place to live. Her choice had been made for her, and she didn't know it yet.

Christian looked over to where she played happily with her dogs. He wished that he could save this moment for her, this last precious sparkling summer afternoon before she had to know that she would soon be bound to a . . . a . . . oh, he didn't even know what to call him. He'd have to consult with Hayes Centaur to beef up his vocabulary.

The unconcerned king and the chancellor of the exchequer finished their game and decided there was time for a nice long nap before dinner. After they'd gone, the servants removed the dirty luncheon plates and the tables and chairs, and swept up. The terrace was empty except for Christian, Marigold, and the dogs.

Should he tell her? Why would she listen to a person she believed was a stranger, who had been at the castle for less than two days, and was a servant as well? She'd think he was a lunatic and have him fired. Then it would be impossible for him to keep an eye on her, just in case Olympia was serious about her accident scheme.

All right, so he wouldn't tell her. But he would stay very, very alert.

The ball rolled away from the dogs and came to rest against Christian's basket of tools. When the barking floor mops came running after it, Christian couldn't help reaching out to pet them from where he knelt next to the wall. He missed Bub and Cate to the point of pain, and at this moment especially, he needed a dog to pet.

The little dogs responded enthusiastically. Maybe no one was willing to touch them, either, because of their connection to Marigold. They leaned against him and licked his hands and jumped up on him.

"Are they bothering you?" Marigold asked, a bit shyly, Christian thought, considering how outspoken she'd been before lunch.

"Not at all," Christian said. "What are their names?"

"Flopsy, Mopsy, and Topsy," she said. "Topsy's the one that got kicked last night."

For a moment they both looked down at the dogs as indulgently as fond parents. Then Marigold said, "So you've read Greek myths?"

"I happen to know about Narcissus," he admitted. "I hope I didn't offend you."

"Not at all. I was merely surprised." She didn't add "... that a servant would know such a thing," but he knew that's what she meant.

"Prince Cyprian must have been asleep during his Greek-myth lessons."

"I know about the style of education in the court of Upper Lower Grevania," Marigold said. "Not rigorous at all. Consequently, Prince Cyprian is an uneducated blockhead without even the sense to know what a moron he is."

Well, he could see he needn't have worried that Cyprian had charmed her.

"Perhaps as Queen of Upper Lower Grevania you could improve their schooling system," Christian said tactfully. He couldn't reveal that he knew Prince Cyprian had withdrawn his offer.

"I have no intention of being Queen of Upper Lower Grevania," she said disdainfully. "I'd rather harvest potatoes for the rest of my life."

"So Sir Magnus will be your choice?" Christian asked carefully.

"That's what my father, the king, would like," the princess said a bit wistfully, "because then I could continue to live here and see him every day. And I love him so much I hate to disappoint him."

Christian waited for the "but," and it soon came.

"But," Marigold went on, "Magnus is so . . . so *meek*. It makes me want to order him around, as if I were his mother. Besides, he kicked Topsy." After a pause, she added, "Oh, I suppose he's harmless enough, and kicking Topsy probably really *was* an accident. But I know what he wants, and it's not me." After another pause she said, "My father has been ill, you know. And he's quite old. I want him to be happy."

Christian couldn't keep his mouth shut. "But what about this morning when you said there was nothing you wanted that you could get by being married?"

She smiled sadly at him. "I forgot about my father's happiness. My marriage could give me that."

"But . . . to *Magnus*?" Christian asked. He knew he'd long ago crossed the line of what was proper for a servant to say to his mistress, but it was harder and harder for him to think of her that way. Because he was already in the danger zone anyway, he decided to keep going. As Ed would say, might as well be hanged for a goat as a cow, whatever that meant. It made even less sense to Christian than most of Ed's sayings.

"There isn't anybody else," she said. "Every eligible royal male for many leagues has been here to have a look at me, and I've rejected them all. A bigger collection of egos, nincompoops, or martinets I've never seen. As well as a few nice young men I just had nothing in common with. And most of them haven't really been interested in me, anyway, since I'm not your traditional princess. Magnus is my last chance."

"Does he have to be royal?" Christian asked. "Is that the part that would make your father happy?"

"I don't think Papa really cares about that. He just wants me to have a good companion for my life. But don't forget about my mother. She's got something to say about it, too. And for her, it has to be a royal suitor or nothing. She'd make my father miserable if he allowed anything else, and then my marriage would be for naught."

This was so complicated, Christian could hardly keep up with it. Luckily, Marigold was smart or she might do something really stupid. Though Chris couldn't quite see how marrying Magnus was the smartest thing to do. Still, Christian was happy that she was talking to him as if he were her equal, someone she could trust with her confidences.

"I have three beautiful sisters, as you probably know," Marigold said, playing with the tassel at the end of her sash, "and they've all married royalty, and they all married for love. Calista and Eve are married to twin brothers, Princes Teddy and Harry of Zandelphia, King Beaufort's kingdom next door. They'll both be queens someday because both brothers will have to be king. When they were infants, they looked so much alike that they got mixed up and nobody knew which was which, so nobody's sure who's the oldest. Imagine what a mess that'll be—two queens and two kings. My other sister, Tatiana, is already Queen of Middle Sanibar. Her husband, King Willie, inherited the throne when he was only fourteen, and he still rules like a well-meaning but birdbrained teenager, if you ask me. Luckily, she's a very sensible person, and he's smart enough to ask her for advice. Their weddings— all on the same day—were a madhouse, but my mother loved it. Every royal personage in this hemisphere was here, packed into every space in the castle, and the feasting was monumental—enough to make you sick. So you can see, even if it was all right with my father, my mother would never permit a commoner son-in-law. She has a reputation to uphold. She always says she wants to be the mother of at least three queens. By that, I guess, she means she isn't convinced I'll make the grade."

Christian sat back on his heels to listen to her. He

couldn't tell her that he had watched her sisters' wedding festivities from across the river, that he knew how she chafed in her finery and had been ignored and avoided by the wedding guests.

He also couldn't tell her that one reason Queen Olympia wasn't convinced Marigold would be a queen was that she might be the one to prevent it.

"If you were queen, how would you rule?" he asked, trying to imagine her in Queen Olympia's place.

"You know," she said, settling down cross-legged on the flagstones, her skirts poufed out around her so that, to Christian, she looked like a flower growing in a fancy pot, "I've thought about that a lot—because ruling means having power, and when you have it, you have to use it wisely. You can't ignore it, the way I'm afraid my dear papa has done, or abuse it the way—well, the way some royals do—and you can't take it for granted, either."

When she talked about abuse, Christian knew she was thinking of her mother, and when she talked about taking it for granted, he was thinking about Queen Mab.

"First of all," she went on, "I'd make sure everybody had a place to live and enough to eat. You can't do anything else well if you're worried every day about that. Then I'd make sure everybody could read.

That way they could learn how to do anything they wanted to do, and they could entertain themselves, too. And I'd make sure everybody had good manners so my kingdom would run smoothly. And that everybody had the right amount of work to do. Too much idleness makes you boring and useless, and too much work makes you bitter and tired."

These were wonderful ideas, Christian thought. He would definitely want to be a subject in any kingdom she ruled.

"What about disciplining people who did bad things?" he asked her. "There are always some."

"That would be the hardest part. I'd hate that. What would you do?"

He was flattered to be asked. And even though he'd never thought about it before, an answer came directly to him, as if it had been sitting in his brain just waiting for him to use it. "I think I'd have a list of punishments for specific crimes, so everybody would know what the consequences would be before they did something bad. And then I'd give the punishments even if I didn't want to, even if the criminal was somebody I knew and liked a lot. That way everybody would know I meant business, and they'd think about it before they did bad things."

Marigold looked admiringly at him. "Well, of

course. That's exactly the right thing to do. Papa just exiles everybody who commits crimes, because he can't bear to think about doing anything worse. And Mother would probably execute them all if she had her way, but she doesn't, so she just yells a lot and then tells Papa to exile them. Even for little things."

"Could I make one suggestion about your rule?" Christian asked, wondering how he had such nerve. But in his pocket was the diamond earring she had given him, still wrapped in her monogrammed handkerchief, so in some basic way, she was just his best friend, not somebody who might one day rule the kingdom in which he was a subject.

"What?" She leaned forward to listen.

"Rewards for good deeds as well as punishments for bad ones. Nobody ever gets enough appreciation when they're behaving themselves, but there's no end to hearing about it when they're not." He wasn't sure how he knew this, since it wasn't something Ed had ever done, but he was sure it was true.

"Absolutely right," she said, nodding. "Oh, figuring out the rewards would be the fun part. There could be chocolate sculptures or golden trophies or talking birds or . . . I'm sorry," she said suddenly, her smile fading. "I shouldn't be going on like this. But somehow I feel like I've known you for a long time.

Aside from my dogs, you're the best listener I've ever known. You ask wonderful questions and really pay attention to the answers, and you don't interrupt, and you think about what I'm saying, and you have good ideas. But I've talked too much and kept you from your work, and I apologize."

Christian stood up, in wonder that a real princess was so unused to being listened to, she would apologize to a house servant when he did. He wanted to touch her, to hold her hand, to give her one of those daily lifesaving hugs he knew she needed. But, of course, he couldn't. Such a thing would probably get him beheaded by sunset.

He did it anyway. He pulled her to her feet and put his arms around her and drew her close to him and just held her, his chin on the top of her head. She smelled wonderful—something floral and spicy at the same time—probably one of her own marvelous concoctions. And she was so soft.

Christian's heartbeat stuttered, and he could imagine a tiny tear appearing in a corner of his heart—a tear that would never heal as long as she was so unhappy and so gallant. And so forbidden to him.

At first she was stiff and shocked. Then she drew a shuddering breath, almost a sob, and relaxed against him. Her hands came up around his back. Neither of them said a word, and neither of them moved.

ED THOUGHT he was going to drop straight down over the waterfall when he looked through the telescope and saw Christian and Princess Marigold embracing. In public, for pete's sake. He didn't even want to *think* about what would happen to a servant who touched a princess like that. How fast would they catch him and put him in the thumbscrews? Or would they just run him through with a sword, on the spot?

Ed's eyes brimmed over. When they'd said good-bye yesterday—only yesterday!—he'd never dreamed it was good-bye forever. He thought of all the things he could have told Christian—*should* have told him—that would have prevented this awful situation. But it was too late now to lock the barn door after the wolf in sheep's clothing was stolen. All he could do was try to figure out some way to help.

He turned to run back to the cave. He needed Walter and Carrie.

11

Marigold was the one who finally broke the embrace. Christian made no attempt to stop her. He had meant only to comfort her, and when it had turned— for him, at least—into something deeper and more complex, he decided that all he could do was enjoy it for as long as it lasted. Because if ever there was a doomed dream, this was it.

"I know what you're thinking, and I wish you were a prince, too," she whispered in a quavery voice, and ran from him, through the archway and down the stairs. Flopsy, Mopsy, and Topsy followed, yapping happily. As wonderful as dogs can be, they are famous for missing the point.

Christian sank back onto his knees and took up his tools again, but he couldn't remember what he was supposed to be doing with them. His head was full of the feel of her, her scent, her voice. He hadn't even worried about her being able to read his thoughts. How could it harm her to know that he thought she was wonderful? It could harm *him*, of course, if she told anyone. But somehow he knew she wouldn't.

He sat idle for a long time before his jumbled thoughts were interrupted by the flutter of wings. He looked up, and there on the wall above him were two pigeons.

"Walter?" he said, surprised. "Carrie?" How did Ed know that p-mail from him was exactly what Chris needed at that moment?

He saw that the message cylinders on all four of their legs were full. Quickly he detached them and unrolled the little pieces of paper. He spread them out on the flagstones and rearranged them until they made sense.

> *Dear Christian, Are you insane? I saw you hugging the princess and I wonder if you have a death wish. You can get beheaded*

———

for that, you know. I forbid you from
touching her again. It is suicide. You need
to leave the castle immediately, before you

get caught. I was wrong to send you out
into the world. You're not ready. This is a
fine kettle of birds of a feather you've

gotten yourself into. Come home right
now.   *Yours, Edric*

He almost laughed. He could tell from the hand-writing that Ed had been hopping up and down as he wrote. It gave him a queer feeling to know that Ed had been watching him through the telescope the same way he himself had watched Princess Marigold.

The birds wouldn't leave until they had an answer to Ed's message, and besides, he needed to tell Ed what was going on here, and to get some advice. The story was so complicated it would take several trips back and forth across the river to get it all told.

Now, where was he going to find writing materials when so few servants knew how to read and write? He'd have to filch some, that's all. But first he'd have to find where to filch them from.

"You stay here," he said to the pigeons. "I'll be back as soon as I can."

He ran down the steps into the castle without any idea of where he was going. He headed down the first hallway he came to, gingerly opening doors and peeking inside. This seemed to be a floor of bedrooms, mostly unoccupied, though he did come upon several people napping, and one tableau of a young man kneeling at a young woman's feet. They both were weeping, and turned wet, startled faces to him as he hastily backed away saying, "Pardon. Pardon. Wrong room."

At the end of the hall was a large room with books enclosed behind glass doors on all four walls. A writing table with ornately carved legs stood in the center of the room, well-stocked with pens, ink, and writing paper. Christian knew he couldn't stand there writing for as long as his tale would take to explain, so he stuffed paper and writing implements into the pockets of his apron. Walking quickly but carefully, so as not to spill the ink, he made it back to the terrace.

He constructed a little barricade of chairs where he was supposed to be working and settled down to scratch out the story for Ed. The pigeons cooed impatiently as they paced along the wall. They'd gotten used to the grain Marigold gave them when they came calling at the castle before, and were quite put out to see that Christian wasn't providing the same treat.

Finally he squeezed what he'd written so far into their message cylinders and sent them back across the river while he continued telling all that he knew about the castle intrigues, three lines at a time.

And every time Walter and Carrie flew across the river, Rollo, watching from up in the barbican, kept track.

THAT EVENING Christian was again in charge of the wine at dinner. Prince Cyprian's retinue made the most of their final banquet, swilling and chomping as if it would be their last meal on earth. Prince Cyprian was having such a grand old time, singing and pinching the serving wenches, that anyone who was paying attention—and Marigold was—could see that he had no regrets.

Swithbert bumbled along having his usual good time, though Christian now knew that the gleam in his eyes came not entirely from the rheuminess of age. The gleam came also from the intelligence and lucidity of a king who might be old and infirm but had lost none of his faculties.

As for Sir Magnus, he was enjoying his peacock

pie and suet pudding with marmalade as if he were already the royal consort.

In the middle of dinner, Queen Olympia stood and banged on her glass with her spoon. In the general din of the extravaganza of eating, the diners didn't even hear her. She tried a few more times without success and then motioned one of the fanfare trumpeters over. A moment later a blast from his instrument stopped everyone, midslurp, midcrunch, or midword.

"Ladies and gentlemen," Olympia said, "and the rest of you, too." She waved her hands to indicate most of the guests. "My husband has an announcement to make." She nodded in King Swithbert's direction.

The king stood, looked around in a bemused manner, and then nodded back in her direction. "You go ahead, my dear," he said, and sat down.

"Very well," she said, adjusting the heavy gold jewelry around her neck. "It gives us great pleasure tonight to announce the engagement of our daughter, Princess Marigold Felicity January Pearl, to Sir Magnus Tobias Hunter. The wedding invitations have gone out to neighboring kingdoms by swift horses, and those of you who are already here are invited to stay. The ceremony will be in three days' time."

The old bat wasn't wasting any time, Christian thought, scrutinizing Marigold for her reaction.

She had turned, aghast, to gape at her mother, and Christian understood that while she had doubtless known she no longer had a choice of suitors, she had known nothing of these hasty wedding plans until that very moment.

The diners burst into applause—no doubt at the prospect of at least three more days of freeloading—and a number of them rushed to congratulate Magnus and Marigold. It did not escape Christian that never once did Magnus look in Marigold's direction, nor she in his. Queen Olympia hadn't been kidding when she said royal marriages weren't based on love.

The tear in the corner of Christian's heart deepened a little.

The evening was excruciatingly long. With more to celebrate, the guests partied harder than ever, dancing on the tabletops and tossing their empty glasses into the huge fireplace. Every broken glass and kicked-over pitcher of wine added to the time the servants would be cleaning up after them.

Christian wondered if he'd be sleeping at all that night. And not just because he'd be so busy with the cleanup.

12

As it turned out, Christian never even got *near* his bed of straw. By the time he had finished sweeping up the shards of glass and the spilled food that littered the Great Hall, the first rays of morning sunlight were coming down through the tall, leaded-glass windows.

He dumped the piles of debris in the dustbin and went to wash his hands before getting back to work. Might as well finish the terrace wall. Might as well throw himself *over* the wall, actually. That, at least, would cure the whopping headache he'd had ever since Queen Olympia had announced Marigold's engagement—a headache made even worse when King Swithbert said how happy he was that Marigold and

Magnus would continue to live in the castle. From the look on the queen's face when he'd said that, Christian could imagine she was thinking about the kinds of accidents that could happen to both Marigold and the king.

He dragged his tool basket up the stairs and went out onto the terrace into the early light. Across the river the spray from the waterfall threw rainbows out over the water, and the dewdrops on the flowers in the terrace pots glittered like diamonds. It was disgustingly glorious.

He dropped his basket of tools and leaned his elbows on the wall, hoping to see Ed looking at him through the telescope, or Walter and Carrie on their way to him with the answer to his prayers. But none of them was anywhere in sight.

Turning his head, he saw Marigold leaning on the wall, way down at the other end of the terrace, still in that awful, overwrought gown. She, apparently, hadn't slept, either. When she turned and saw him, their eyes held for a long, expressive moment. She lifted her hand and wiggled her fingers at him. He lifted his hand, too, and then knew what he had to do.

Christian ran the length of the terrace and pulled her into his arms. "You can't marry Magnus," he exclaimed, throwing restraint to the winds. "You can't. It will kill you."

She laid her head against his chest and hugged him back. "I know," she said. "But what else can I do?"

"You can run away with me." He almost looked over his shoulder to see who had spoken those words, they came so unexpectedly out of his mouth. Oh well. Might as well be a goat as a cow. Or whatever. "You can bring the dogs. My dogs would love that. You'd never have to wear one of these"—he swatted at the floppy bow on the gown's shoulder—"again."

He felt her smile against his chest. "That is the nicest offer anyone has ever made to me," she said. "But it's impossible. It would break Papa's heart. And it would guarantee my mother would be the ruler of the kingdom."

"She's going to be ruler anyway," Christian said. Maybe he'd have been more circumspect if he wasn't light-headed from fear and lack of sleep, but he wasn't sure. "I wasn't kidding when I said marrying Magnus would kill you. I overheard your mother talking to that ferret of hers, and she wants you out of her way— and your father, too. As in *fatal accident*. Then she's going to pack Magnus off to his own manor, and she gets to be sole ruler."

He held his breath, waiting for her to call for some soldiers to take him away for committing treason.

Marigold looked up at him, astonished. "My own mother is thinking this? Are you sure?"

"Pretty sure," he said, not loosening his hold on her. It was too late to back up now. "Sure enough to make me think it would be a good idea for you to get out of here until she can be stopped."

"Well, my goodness," Marigold said. "I wish I could say I don't believe you." Resting her head against his heart, she sighed deeply. Then, after a moment, she raised her head, looked into his eyes, and smiled a perfectly dazzling smile. "I should have known it was you. When I first touched you, I could tell you were thinking... well... warm thoughts about me. But I didn't realize it was really *you*. Somehow I never thought we'd actually meet. I thought we'd still be p-mailing even when I was an old lady, married off in some distant kingdom. Imagine me finding you right now when I need you the most. Can't you tell me your real name now?"

Relief filled him. She knew him! He could be her best friend again with no more pretending. "First, I want you to know how awful I've felt about having had to deceive you," he told her. "We promised never to lie or deceive, but I just couldn't, as a commoner, insist that a princess honor a best-friend promise, especially to a servant."

"Oh, don't you know friendship pays no attention to things like that? The heart doesn't care about anything except loyalty and comfort and companionship—which you've always given me and are still giving me. Now, please—it's unfair that you know my name and I don't know yours."

"It's Christian. You had it right one time out of six—and those were my favorite p-mails."

"I'm so glad it isn't Chauncey! You just never seemed like a Chauncey."

"How did you know it's me?"

"Because you're being my bulwark. The way my best friend promised to be."

"So you figured it out for yourself? You didn't read my mind?"

"I can only get thoughts and feelings, not names and addresses."

"I can't imagine thinking something I wouldn't want you to know anyway."

She lowered her eyes. "To tell the truth, I can't always do it. It only works when I'm unhappy. That's the part of the curse nobody knows about. And, of course, I've been sufficiently unhappy growing up here that I could do it often enough to scare people pretty badly. The first time it happened, I was only about four and my mother was dragging me back to the nursery because I'd interrupted her while she was playing whist with some of her ladies-in-waiting. I said to her, 'Do you *really* wish I'd never been born?' and she dropped my hand as if it were on fire and said, 'How did you do that?' So I knew, somehow, that I'd read her private thoughts. It happened a couple more times before she figured out it only happened when she was touching me. So she stopped. And pretty soon, everybody else did, too. Even my governess. Everybody except Papa. He was never afraid of me. But, then, he never had any thoughts that would bother me. And usually, I was happy around him, so I couldn't read him anyhow."

"I think you should grab hold of your mother and make sure what I'm afraid she's up to is really true. And if it is, you have to get out of here. You can stay with me and Ed if you want. Or go to one of your sisters. Then we can keep p-mailing the way you want. But I have to know you're safe."

"Is that really so important to you?"

The way she was looking at him made him feel quite jingle-brained—she would have fun reading *those* thoughts. "Yes," he said after shaking his head to clear his mind. "I can hardly think of anything that matters more."

"I believe you," she said. "And now I'm losing your thoughts."

"Why? Because . . . because . . . you're happy?" He hardly dared hope that his concern for her would make her too happy to read his thoughts.

"I know it seems crazy to be happy to find out that my own mother wants me out of her way permanently. But by finding that out, I've also found out that my best friend is here and that he—" She blushed prettily and lowered her lashes. "I was so glad when you started writing to me," she whispered. "It was exactly what I needed then."

"I knew I was being very forward that day, but somehow I couldn't help myself. I was just so curious about what you were reading. I admit I was surprised when you answered me."

"So was I. But you couldn't know how lonely I was when you sent me that first message, how much I wanted a friend."

"Well, now you have one," he said, and hugged her again, wishing that right now she *could* read his thoughts and know that he wanted to be much more than just a friend to her.

At that moment, a platoon of castle soldiers, led by Rollo, burst up the stairs and out onto the terrace.

"Halt!" Rollo cried.

Christian and Marigold sprang apart. Was Rollo talking to them or to his soldiers?

"Take him!" Rollo said, and Christian found himself pinioned by more soldiers than he could count, all of them bristling with weapons.

"Stop it!" Marigold demanded. "I'm the princess here, and I command you to stop!"

"Sorry, princess," Rollo said. "You're outranked by the queen, whose orders I'm carrying out."

"But what have I done?" Christian asked.

"Aside from mauling a royal personage, you mean?" Rollo asked, and Christian could see in his eyes that it didn't really matter what he'd done, or how many excuses he had, or how many witnesses there might be to his good character. Rollo was going to get even for the incident with Meg in the kitchen.

"He wasn't mauling me!" Marigold exclaimed, stamping her foot.

"That's what it looked like to me!" Rollo said. "But that's not the real problem here."

"Well, what is?" she asked.

"This man is a traitor, plotting the invasion of the castle."

"What?" Marigold and Christian said in unison.

"He's been seen sending many messages to a confederate across the river. His only purpose in coming to work here has been to report back to his forces how they could breach the walls and capture the kingdom."

"Why, that's total nonsense!" Christian cried. "I don't have any forces."

"Total nonsense," Marigold repeated. "You saw me touching him. You know I can tell what he's thinking, and nothing like that was in his mind."

"I'm just following my orders, Your Highness," Rollo said. "I'm sure you'll get a chance to have your say at his trial. You, too," he threw in Christian's direction. "Before they hang you," he muttered. Then, louder, to his soldiers, "Take him away. To the lowest dungeon. And bring me the key."

Christian was dragged away backward, his heels scraping along the flagstones.

Marigold ran after him. "Don't despair," she cried. "He can't do this. I'll get you out in no time."

13

"No time" apparently meant never, Christian thought, languishing in his dank, cluttered dungeon. He didn't know how long he'd been there, for it was hard to judge the passage of time without a window to the outside. The sputtering torch in the wall bracket across from his cell burned all the time.

The cell was spacious, with room for perhaps thirty prisoners. At the moment, it was more than half filled with junk, presumably from the blacksmith's unsuccessful inventions. Christian could see chains and manacles screwed into the walls where unfortunate former inmates had been bound, and was grateful he at least had the freedom to wander around in his dark confinement.

He soon discovered that in even a spacious dungeon there wasn't much wandering to be done. His back against the wall, he slid into a sitting position on the damp floor, and before he knew it, his sleepless night caught up with him and he was out like a log.

He woke to the sound of someone whispering his name.

"Christian!" the voice hissed. "Wake *up*!"

He jumped to his feet and went to the small barred window in the thick wooden door of the cell. In the dimly lit square was Marigold's face. Christian had never seen a more beautiful sight.

"Hi," he said, ecstatic simply to lay eyes on her.

"Oh, Christian," she wailed. "I've tried to talk to Papa, but he's so fuddled I can only assume that my mother has drugged him to keep him from making any trouble until after this awful wedding's over. Maybe she's been drugging him for a long time, which is why he's seemed so ill and old."

"Then save yourself," Christian said decisively. "Forget about me. I'll think of something. But you've got to get out of here. You can't marry Magnus. You can't."

"I'm being watched all the time now," Marigold said. "There are two guards at either end of the corridor right now, and they'll escort me back to my rooms. Then my maids will watch me, with guards at the doors and windows. The only way I could get out of here would be if I had wings."

"But they're letting you come see me," he said. "Why?"

"I suppose they're hoping you'll tell me about your plot to overthrow the king, or whatever crazy charges they've trumped up against you. If they can get you to confess, they won't even have to bother with a trial."

"There *is* no plot, you know that. I was just sending p-mail to Ed across the river."

"I do know that. I haven't doubted you for a minute."

"We have two more days before the wedding. Maybe I can think of something. And even if I can't, as long as you can come to see me here, I'll die happy."

"Oh, don't talk like that." Marigold's eyes swam with tears.

He put his hands over hers where they gripped the bars, and squeezed. "We have to be realistic. But let's not cry yet."

"Princess!" one of the guards called. "Your time's up. You have to go now."

He squeezed her hands again. "Come back," he whispered.

"I will." Then she was gone.

Christian slumped to the floor, completely out of ideas just when he was most desperate for a good one.

He realized that he'd dozed again when he was awakened by a terrible racket coming down the corridor. Christian couldn't distinguish a single word of the shouts and the clamor of many voices that rang off the stone walls. And he thought he heard dogs barking.

There was a rattle of keys. The cell door was flung open and a tumble of flailing bodies was hurled inside. Christian pressed himself against the wall to avoid being struck by flying humanity while noting that apparently Rollo didn't have the only key. The whizzing bodies hit the ground with a crash followed by grunts and yips and groans. What in the world kind of creatures were in here now? Christian wondered with trepidation.

The heap on the floor sorted itself out into three distinct shapes, two of which launched themselves directly at him. At the moment of impact, Christian discerned that they were—Bub! And Cate! And behind them, brushing himself off, was Ed!

"Ed!" Chris cried. Even encumbered as he was by the dogs, he threw himself on Ed, trying to hug all three of them at the same time.

"Help!" Ed cried. "Get off me!"

Bub barked his brains out directly into Chris's ear, and Cate howled and yowled and flung herself about.

"It's me—Christian!" Chris yelled over the tumult.

Ed pulled himself back out of the melee. "Christian?" he sputtered. When he'd assured himself that it was indeed Christian, he threw his arms around him. "Thank goodness you're still alive! Are you in here because you hugged the princess?"

"Did you get all my p-mail?" Christian asked.

"I think so. Lots and lots of little pieces of paper. I was hopping up and down waiting for the next twelve lines."

"Then you know what's going on here. And now they think all those messages we were sending were something about planning an attack on the castle."

"You're joking," Ed said, ready to laugh. "Two guys and two dogs were going to attack the castle?"

"I'm not joking. That's why we're all in here. But it also prevents us from interfering with Princess Marigold's wedding to that oaf, that brainless boob, Magnus."

"You don't like Magnus, huh?" Ed asked.

"Well, I told you all that in the messages. And every time I think of him with Marigold, I—well, I feel a way I've never felt before. A way so strong it hurts, right in the corner of my heart."

Uh-oh, thought Ed. He'd felt that way himself, and he knew what it meant. He felt that way every year at the LEFT Conference when he saw the red-haired troll maiden. From time to time she smiled at him, but whenever she did, she was dragged off by her father, who wanted better for her than a common forest troll who lived off other people's castoffs and didn't have an ODD Medal. And every year at the conference, he had to brace himself before he found out whether she'd gotten married since he last saw her. So far she hadn't, but the conference was coming up again in a week. So he knew what a breaking heart felt like.

"We have to stop that wedding," Christian said. "We have to."

"Any suggestions?" Ed inquired. "We're not exactly in a good position to do that."

"I know it looks bad right now—"

"*Bad?*" Ed said. "You know that saying about how it's always darkest just after the lights go out? That's what it looks like to me."

"No, I don't know that saying," Christian said.

"But I'm not giving up as long as I have a breath in my body." He gestured to the scrap heap. "Look at all that junk. Maybe there's something in there we can use."

"Use for what?" Ed asked. "I hate to be a wet blanket in the mud, but haven't you noticed? We're locked in."

"Don't be so negative. Help me look." Christian began digging into the pile, running to the little window in the door for enough light to see everything he dug up.

14

In Marigold's chamber were two dressmakers, four maids, one page boy, three dogs, one ferret, and her mother. While Marigold was the focus of all their attentions, it was the *princess*, not the *person* preoccupying everyone.

"No!" Olympia cried, pacing around her daughter, with Fenleigh, growling softly, clutched under her arm. Flopsy, Mopsy, and Topsy growled back, wishing they could get that creature away from Olympia for just a few minutes. "No bows on the front! I want them all on the back! Pearls and brilliants and lace and embroidery on the front. Bows on the back. Can't you get that straight?" She snatched a bow pinned to the bodice of the wedding gown and threw it onto the floor.

One of the dressmakers, her lips compressed as if she were struggling not to bite Olympia, picked up the bow and fastened it at the back of Marigold's waist.

"*Much* better," purred Olympia. Fenleigh purred, too. "Now the veil—"

And so it went, all afternoon, with Marigold nothing more than a breathing mannequin for everybody in the room. But she was doing more than breathing. She was *thinking*.

How to stop this wedding? How to free Christian? How to find a way to go see Christian again in the dungeon? Was it really drugs—or worse: *poison*—that were making Papa so befuddled and vague?

Lots of questions. No answers. Except how she would see Christian again. She just *would*, that's all. She was a princess, wasn't she? And a future queen. And she knew how to act like one.

"Enough," she said. "I've stood here long enough while you've treated me like a pincushion. This dress is getting even uglier, and I can't stand to wear it for one more instant." She began pulling it off her shoulders, pins and bows popping everywhere. The alarmed seamstresses scurried around her, trying to minimize the damage.

"Oh, Marigold," her mother said impatiently. "Stop that! You're ruining this gown and you're acting like a child. You have a duty to do, and I'm here to see that you do it. Now, behave yourself."

"I should remind you," Marigold said, stepping out of the dress on the floor and standing in her chemise and petticoat, "that you're talking to the future queen. And I won't be spoken to that way."

"Well!" Olympia huffed. And then, with steel in her voice, "We'll just see about that. And let *me* remind *you* that you're speaking to the *present* queen, and *I* won't be spoken to *that* way."

They faced off while the seamstresses and maids, dogs and page boy, took careful, silent steps backward until they bumped against the walls.

"I'm not marrying Magnus," Marigold said firmly. "I know it would make Papa happy, and I know it's something you want, too, albeit for reasons completely different from his, but I won't do it. He's unacceptable to me."

"I don't know what you can mean," Olympia said. "He's a very handsome man, and you're lucky that, plain as you are, you can get *any* man interested in you. As for my reasons for wanting you to marry Magnus, I have no idea what you're talking about. Your future well-being is my only concern." She took a quick look around at her audience, a look that said: Can you believe what this silly girl is saying?

"My future well-being is even more of a concern for me than it is for you," Marigold said, "and that's why I'm not marrying Magnus." She reached out and grabbed her mother's hands, holding tightly even when her mother tried to pull away. Then Marigold gasped, snatched her dressing gown from the hands of the startled page, and dashed out the door. As she ran down the long carpeted hallway in her stocking feet, past the guards, pulling her dressing gown on as she went, she could hear Olympia's voice behind her. "Prewedding jitters, that's all. Just ignore her. But"— and her voice raised—"follow her!"

Marigold heard the guards running to keep up, but she didn't slow down. She ran all the way to the dungeon.

Christian was under the window, holding something up for identification—a spring? a ratchet?— when Marigold's face appeared, blocking his light.

"Precious!" he exclaimed. He thought he heard Ed groan behind him.

Chris couldn't know how long Marigold had wished for someone besides her papa to call her that. Her heart melted and then froze right up again, like a pond in the terrible kingdom of Isobaria, where the temperature never could make up its mind.

Loving a doomed person was a pretty foolish thing to do. She knew that, but she couldn't seem to help it. She pressed her hand to her chest. It felt as if a tear had opened in the corner of her heart.

"Are you all right?" she asked.

"I'm fine," he said, without adding, "so far." "I've even got company. Ed and Bub and Cate are here."

"Here? What are they doing here?"

"Rollo went over and found them. Because of that invasion we're planning, you know."

"Oh no! I'm so sorry."

"Sorry? I'm glad. They're my family. I've missed them terribly." Their fingers entwined through the cell's bars. "Are you all right?" Christian's voice softened.

"Yes. Now." She gazed at him and said sadly, "You should see my wedding gown. You'd hate it."

"I'd hate anything you wore to be married to Magnus."

"I'm not going to marry him," she declared.

"You're not? How will you avoid it?" Hope rose cautiously in his heart. "Have you figured out a way to run away?"

"I don't know how I'll avoid it," she said. "I'm still thinking. I just know I can't do it. I'd rather be dead. And you were right about my mother. I touched her hands—and now she knows I know."

"Then you're in more danger than ever," Christian said, alarmed.

"I don't care." Marigold's chin trembled. "Maybe then you and I can be together. Remember Andromeda and Perseus up in the sky, together forever?"

"I'd rather be together on the ground. You're not forgetting, are you, that I'm only a servant, the ward of a forest troll, with nothing to offer a princess?"

"Why should you offer anything but yourself?" she replied a bit tartly. "That's what I'm most interested in. I've already got everything else any sensible person could want. *More* doesn't mean better. *Enough* is as good as a feast, you know."

"That's what Ed always says. Or, what he says is, too much of a good thing is as good as a feast, but that's what he means. I think. With Ed it's sometimes hard to know. But, of course, I don't want you to marry Magnus any more than you want to. There's a solution, I'm sure there is, so don't worry."

She shook her head in disbelief, a faint smile on her lips. "Don't worry?" she repeated.

"Oh, I know it looks serious, but what good is worrying? It just gets in the way of thinking."

"Marigold!" came her mother's imperious voice. "I forbid you to speak to that traitorous servant. Come here this instant."

Marigold tightened her grip on the bars. "If I ever get to be a queen, I'm never going to use that tone of voice with anybody."

"You don't think being imperious is one of the requirements for being a queen?" Christian asked.

"Certainly not," Marigold replied. "It doesn't work, anyway. It just makes people feel worthless, and then they get angry. And eventually you've got a rebellion on your hands. My mother's been talking to me that way all my life and I can tell you, *I'm* angry. *I'm* ready for a rebellion." She turned to look at her mother standing at the top of the stairs, Fenleigh on a leash at her feet. "I'm not coming!" she shouted. "And I'm not marrying Magnus."

"That's what you think," the queen said. She pointed an extremely imperious finger at Marigold and said to the guards nearest her, "Lock her up." And then, to the guard standing a ways down the corridor, "Help them if she tries to get away."

Before Marigold knew what was happening, she

was grabbed from behind, wrested away from her hold on the bars to Christian's cell, and pulled backward to the cell next door.

Christian heard the key rattle in the lock, accompanied by sounds of struggle and of Marigold saying, "I will *not* go! I will *not*!"

But, of course, she did. The strongest will in the world is no match for brute force, whatever satisfaction may be gained from having resisted. Christian heard the cell door bang shut and the keys rattle again as Marigold's voice became muffled, even as she kept refusing to go.

"I'll be back to let you out an hour before the wedding," Olympia said. "You can even get dressed in there. I'm not taking any chances on you messing this up." She pointed at a guard. "You stay here. One guard will be enough to keep things under control down here. I need the rest of you to come upstairs and keep a lid on the partying. Some of those wedding guests are getting quite out of hand."

"Send Papa to see me!" Marigold called. "I must see Papa!"

"We're not going to disturb your father with this little problem." Olympia's voice faded as she turned her back and walked away. "He's old and tired and needs his rest. Fenleigh thinks so, too."

"Get him down here!" Marigold yelled.

"Sorry," Olympia said gaily, and then the heavy door to the dungeon clanged behind her and her guards.

There was silence for a moment before Christian said, "Marigold, I'd like you to meet Ed. Ed, say hello to Marigold."

"Your Majesty," Ed said meekly.

"Oh, for heaven's sake," Marigold said from next door. "Call me Marigold."

It was strange for Christian to talk to her when he couldn't see her, but it reminded him of all the years when he'd watched her through his telescope and imagined knowing her. And of the year of their p-mail correspondence. He'd talked to her then, in his imagination, when she was almost too far away to be seen. This was better. He could hold her image in his mind while he spoke. And she could answer.

"How about *Princess* Marigold?" Ed suggested. "I've lived a very quiet forest life, and I've suddenly got a lot of new things to get used to. I don't want to push my own self even farther out of my comfort zone."

"All right," Marigold said. "But don't forget I'm pretty far outside my comfort zone, too." She made sure the guard was down the hall, out of earshot, before asking, "Do we have any ideas about how we're going to get out of here?"

"Chris is working on something. Maybe." Ed tried to be reassuring. "We've got some time."

THEY WERE so far down in the bowels of the castle that they could get no hint of what time it was or what was happening above them.

It was this: a three-ring circus of cooking in the vast kitchens to feed the throngs of royalty pouring in from scattered kingdoms, as well as efforts to cook ahead for the blowout, every-man-for-himself, all-you-can-eat feeding frenzy that would occur on the wedding day itself.

A polka dance of maids, domestic and imported, do-si-do-ing between bedchambers, trying to keep up with the gowning, hairdressing, and miscellaneous grooming needs of the flocks of women guests.

A hurricane-flapping of fans by a phalanx of young page boys to keep at bay the clouds of smoke from items—pipes, cigars, and hookahs—in use by the gentlemen wedding guests as they clustered around the billiard tables, library corners, and brandy bottles scattered throughout the castle.

A symphony of nail pounding as the castle carpenters hurried to construct extra tables and benches for the outdoor reception, gazebos for the ceremony and the cutting of the wedding cake, and collapsible tenting to be popped up like a giant umbrella over all the guests on the terrace in case of bad weather on the wedding day.

As far as Ed, Christian, and Marigold were concerned, it was already a very bad weather day.

15

Christian's experiments came to naught. He'd tried building a battering ram from old metal parts, but it fell apart as soon as it hit the door. He'd tried to cut a hole in the door with a rusty saw, which had crumbled to orange dust in his hand. He'd tried to take the hinges off the door with a bent lever, which snapped in two on the first try.

"There's plenty more stuff in the pile," he said, trying to keep his voice bright. "I'll find something I can use."

Bub raised his great shaggy head from his paws and uttered a thin whine. Ed sat on the floor, resting against the damp wall, Cate's trembling muzzle in his lap. He stroked her ears and murmured to her, for once not considering her emoting to be an exaggeration. Personally, he thought Chris was barking up a dead tree.

"Oh, I wish I could see what you have in your pile," Marigold said. "Maybe I could think of something."

"I could describe some things to you."

"Total waste of time," Ed grumbled. "No point to that." He sighed. "I'll never get a share of the tooth fairy business now. Mab'll go on being inefficient and disappointing little children every night, and all the support I was gathering for a showdown at the conference next week will have been for nothing. When I don't show up, nobody'll know what happened to me. And nobody else will take up my cudgel and mantle and challenge her." He sighed again, a gusty, despairing sigh.

"Please, Ed," Christian said, "I wish you'd try to keep a more positive attitude. We're not finished yet." He rummaged through the pile until he found a new piece, then carried it to the door and held it to the light. "Marigold, I have a thing about a foot and a half long with a wheel on one end and a two-pronged gizmo on the other. Any ideas?"

"No," she said. "But go get another thing. I think the trick will be to build something, not to use the pieces individually. So we have to find pieces that'll fit together."

He found another part. "All right. Here's one that's thick and round like a wheel with no spokes. It has two little holes in the middle and hooks all around the outside edges."

"Will the two prongs on the first thing fit into the two holes in the middle of this thing?" Marigold asked.

Christian tried it. "Yes!" he said triumphantly. "It *does* fit!"

"Wonderful," Ed grumbled. "Now you have a bigger thing that still doesn't do anything. Don't you know we're up against a creek with no paddle?" But he remembered how stubborn Chris had been as a child, so he didn't really expect him to pay attention. And Christian didn't.

Hours later, when a guard came with the thin gruel and hard bread that were passing for breakfast—or maybe supper—Christian and Marigold had put together a construction as big as a catapult that looked like nothing anybody had ever seen before. But all the parts seemed to fit together as if they had been designed to do so, and it was hard to resist continuing to build something that appeared to have a purpose, even if they couldn't figure out what that purpose might be.

As they ate their gruel and bread, Christian studied the contraption he'd built. "It looks like it should move," he said to Ed. "Like it's some kind of vehicle."

"You'd need a horse to pull it," Ed commented. "And we got no horse."

"I don't think this thing is supposed to be pulled," Christian said. "I think it's supposed to move under its own power. I just don't know what its power is."

"Bunch of nonsense," Ed muttered into his gruel.

"Marigold," Christian called. "Tell me every way you can think of to make things go."

"There's only pushing or pulling," she said. "Or throwing. Things can be pushed by people or horses or mules or oxen. Things can be pulled by people or horses or mules or oxen. Or dogs, I suppose. Dogs aren't good at pushing, but they can pull."

Christian sat up suddenly and snapped his fingers. "Dogs!" he said, closely examining Bub and Cate who, seeing his look, gave each other a quick glance and began skulking off to a dark corner of the cell. "Oh no, you don't," he said, getting up to go after them.

MAGNUS WAS HAVING tea with Olympia and Fenleigh. "What if she says 'I don't' when it's time for her to say 'I do'?"

"I wouldn't put it past her," Olympia said speculatively, giving Fenleigh a triangular liver-salad sandwich,, which he took in one gulp with a sinister snapping of teeth. "I'll tell her it'll cause her father to collapse or something. That should work."

"How is Uncle Swithbert?" Magnus asked. "I've always been dreadfully fond of him, you know. But he didn't look so good yesterday."

"He's very tired, the poor dear," Olympia said, with only the slightest hollow ring to her sympathetic tone. "I'm giving him something to help him rest. He'll need all his strength for the big day."

"You know, I heard Marigold could read people's minds, but I've touched her, and she doesn't seem to know what I'm thinking. Though I *have* tried to keep my mind full of pleasant, pure thoughts."

"I'm sure they've been totally sterilized," Olympia said, offering him a plate of eel-paste sandwiches. "Completely drained of all their juice."

She looked over at him, thinking what a shame it was that his handsome head was so completely unoccupied. It never even occurred to her that his handsome head truly was filled with pleasant bland thoughts. Still, she considered Magnus's head a lovely change from Swithbert's old gray one, which, unfortunately, had plenty in it, no matter what a bumbler he might appear. This was why he had needed so much of her special sedative for so long, and why he'd needed even more lately to make sure he didn't cause any trouble. She'd always known Marigold was his pet, and she wasn't taking any chances.

KING SWITHBERT lay on his pillow with his eyes closed. But he wasn't asleep. His brain and his ears were in full gear. He was thinking about how the potted frankincense tree in the corner of his bedchamber had dropped all its leaves in the two days he'd been watering it with the tonics Olympia brought him twice a day. And how much better he'd been feeling since the poor tree had taken a turn for the worse.

The last thing he'd heard very clearly from his bed was the sound of Marigold running down the hallway—his precious Marigold, the favorite of his daughters, even though he knew he shouldn't have a favorite. But the others had always seemed so foreign to him, so overwhelming, the three of them together all the time, so hard to know individually. Marigold and he, somehow they understood each other.

He'd heard heavy footsteps running after Marigold, too, which worried him. She was running *from* something, but it was following her. She was unhappy, and that hurt him. He could feel a tear begin in the corner of his heart when he thought of his precious Marigold so miserable.

Could he have made a mistake about Magnus? He'd seemed a harmless sort of chap, not too bright, but pleasant enough. Someone who could be a nice companion for Marigold, a good consort who wouldn't give her any problems and who would be grateful to have a home at last. Magnus had been a pathetic sort of little boy, orphaned early and passed around from relative to relative, always an outsider, drawing all those intricate maps. Swithbert knew that was Magnus's way of trying to find a place of his own in the world. Lucky for him he was a good-looking boy, which made him more acceptable among his royal relatives. And he'd always been so desperately eager to please, always looking for someone who wanted him, who would take his side. Swithbert had wanted to give him a home and family of his own at last. But maybe Marigold wouldn't feel so charitable about that when she was the one who had to be the actual sacrifice.

Still, he'd hoped that Magnus and Marigold might each fill the loneliness in the other. Because as much as he loved Marigold and admired her heart and her mind and her spunk, he knew she'd been a lonely girl, rebuffed by her mother and overlooked by everyone else when she was compared to the busy pack of her sisters. He didn't understand why everybody called her plain. To him, she was beautiful, but maybe that was because he could tell what her soul looked like.

As for her birth-gift, or her curse as some called it, well, he could see how it would bother other people, but it had never been a problem for him. It made him wonder what was going on in Olympia's mind, the way she had avoided touching Marigold for so many years. And what was she up to that she was so determined to keep him out of the way? What was it she was worried he might interfere with?

The king opened one eye. The maid assigned to watch over him was dozing in her chair, her mending sliding off her lap onto the floor.

He opened his other eye and sat up just as Denby, his valet, came into the bedchamber from the dressing room. Denby's eyebrows went up and his mouth fell open. Before he could say a word, Swithbert put a finger to his own lips, then beckoned him to come closer.

Denby came to the side of the bed, and Swithbert whispered into his ear, "Where's Marigold?"

Denby straightened up, conflict written all over his face.

Swithbert put his hands on his hips and glared at Denby, looking as frighteningly regal as it's possible to look in a wrinkled nightshirt with one's hair all rumpled up.

He mouthed: "Don't forget I'm the king around here."

Sighing, Denby bent down and said, "She's in the dungeon. Queen Olympia said she'd put me down there, too, if I told you."

"What?" Swithbert squeaked.

The maid stirred in her chair and then settled back into slumber, snoring in a ladylike manner.

Swithbert swung his legs over the side of the bed and pattered off to the dressing room, motioning for Denby to follow. He yanked a pair of breeches out of the cupboard and, hopping on one foot and then the other as he pulled them on, said, "What the heck's she doing in the dungeon? What's going on around here? Why doesn't Olympia get her out?" He fastened his pants, tucking his nightshirt into them as he shoved his feet into his shoes.

Denby cleared his throat, looking desperately uncomfortable.

"Well?" Swithbert insisted.

Denby cleared his throat again and said in a little

voice, as if he could make his answer smaller, too, "Um. Queen Olympia's the one who put her there."

"This is outrageous!" Swithbert fumed. "Why on earth would her own mother...well, *we're* going to get Marigold out. Let's go."

Swithbert strode out the rear door of the dressing room into the passageway, the tail of his nightshirt hanging out of his pants, with Denby scurrying along behind him.

16

The dungeon guard gaped and almost dropped his broadax. "Sire?" he stammered.

"Open the doors," Swithbert demanded. "And get out of my way."

"But, sire," the guard said, doing a little rumba of indecision, "Queen Olympia said no one's to come down here but her."

Swithbert drew himself up to his full height, which, though it wasn't very high, was enough to intimidate the guard. "*I'm* the king, in case you've forgotten, and my voice is bigger than hers. Now open those doors, or you'll be replacing my daughter in there." There are times, many of them, in which it is an advantage to appear addled, but this wasn't one of them.

The doors were flung open, and the guard rumbaed out of the way so fast he almost fell down.

Swithbert scampered down the stairs and hurried into the corridor, calling, "Marigold! Marigold! It's Papa. Where are you?"

"Papa!" came Marigold's voice. "I'm in here."

"Where's that guard?" Swithbert demanded of Denby. "Get him in here with the keys. We're staging a jailbreak."

"Not just me, Papa. I'm not in here alone."

"God's nightgown!" Swithbert said. "There hasn't been anybody in these cells for years, and now they're filling up. What's Olympia been up to while I've been in a fog? Who else is in here?"

"There's Christian, from the forest. And his foster father, Edric. And two dogs."

"Dogs?" Swithbert said. "My stars, Olympia's lost her marbles."

The guard came along, his arm in Denby's clutches. Swithbert yanked the key ring off his belt so violently that the buckle snapped and his uniform breeches headed south.

"Hey!" the guard yelped, dropping his broadax and grabbing his pants.

Swithbert unlocked Marigold's cell, and she fell into his arms. The king, looking over her shoulder, spotted the bowl of gruel that Marigold had been unable to eat.

"What the heck is that?" he asked.

"Gruel," she said. "It's what prisoners get to eat."

"It doesn't even look like it could be food," he said. "Come on. We're getting you something real to eat."

"You've got to let Chris out, too. And Ed, and the dogs."

"Now, sweetheart," Swithbert said, "you're not going to like this, but we'll have to leave them here. For the time being."

"Why?" demanded Marigold. "They haven't done anything."

"I'm going to have enough trouble keeping your breakout a secret from Olympia while I try to find out what's going on. I don't know how I can keep two more people—and some *dogs*, for heaven's sake—a secret. And I don't have time to figure it out. We have to get out of here *now*. But I promise you, I will come back for them just as soon as this mess is all straightened out."

"I'm not leaving Christian in here."

Swithbert seemed not to hear her. "Denby," he directed, "put this guard in Marigold's cell and then go see if the coast is clear. Tell the captain of the guards—Rollo, isn't it?—that you'll be the one bringing meals to the prisoners and coordinating the guard schedule. Nobody, including Rollo, has to know there won't be any guards. That way no one will know Marigold's gone." He stepped over to Christian and Ed's cell. "If my Marigold vouches for you, that's good enough for me. But you'll have to stay here just a little longer."

"*No,* Papa," Marigold insisted, holding on to the bars of Christian's cell. "They have to get out *now.*"

Christian reached through the bars to run his finger along the smooth curve of her cheek. "It's all right. I'll be waiting for you. Don't forget me."

"Never," she said.

Oh my, thought Ed and Swithbert simultaneously.

Then Marigold and her father were gone. The only sound in the dungeon was the muttering of the guard in the next cell.

"Dang," he said. "The king broke my belt, and now I can't keep my britches on lest I hold them up with both hands."

As Marigold and Swithbert hurried along the palace corridors, Marigold informed her father, "We're going to go to Mother and tell her I'm not marrying Magnus, not on a bet, and that all the wedding guests should go home."

"You don't want to marry Magnus?" Swithbert was a bit breathless.

"I'd rather be boiled in oil. The kind with cholesterol," she said. "I'd rather be hanged by my thumbs. I'd rather be burned at the stake. I'd rather—"

"All right, all right," Swithbert said. "I get it. But why? What's wrong with Magnus? He's always seemed pleasant enough, and I know how much he needs love."

"That's the problem. I *don't* love him. I know that's not a requirement for royal marriages, but I . . . well, I *can't* love him. I love somebody else."

"Somebody else?" But he wasn't as surprised as he made himself sound. He'd seen the looks that passed between Marigold and Christian. "Marigold, my dear," King Swithbert said, putting his arms around his baby, who suddenly seemed more grown-up than he was quite ready to let her be, "have I ever done anything to hurt you, or that wasn't in your best interest?" Even though he could see the handwriting on the wall, he wanted for just a little while longer to be the most important fellow in her life.

"Magnus—," she began.

"Besides Magnus," Swithbert said. "And that was from an apparently misguided concern about both of you."

"No," she had to admit. "You've never done anything to hurt me."

"And I won't now. Trust me. We'll get this straightened out."

BACK IN THE KING'S CHAMBERS, Denby smuggled Swithbert into bed while Marigold hid in the dressing room. Swithbert lay propped on his pillows, enjoying his enactment of a conked-out old geezer, while Denby awakened the maid and dismissed her, saying that he was perfectly capable of looking after someone who did nothing but sleep.

"But Queen Olympia says I'm to stay here," the maid wailed. "She won't like it if I don't. And you know how she can be when she's not happy."

"Then you tell her to come speak to me," Denby said.

"Oh, Denby," the maid answered. "I don't think you know what you're in for—no, you don't."

"You just tell her that. Now go along."

"She'll be coming in herself this evening to give His Majesty his bedtime drink, don't forget."

"No, indeed," Denby said solemnly, while Swithbert tried to keep from laughing at the lovely trick he was playing on Olympia.

After Marigold had finished telling him the whole

story of her p-mailing with Christian and of the plot Olympia had in mind and how it affected the two of them, he no longer felt so jolly.

"I knew she never loved me," he said sadly. "That's how a lot of marriages—not just royal ones—start out, though often love grows, and I'd hoped for that. But I never thought she'd want to do me in. Or you, her own daughter. That's dreadful. And wicked."

"What are we going to do, Papa?"

"You can rest assured you won't be marrying Magnus tomorrow, that's the first thing. And your friend Christian will be getting a medal for uncovering the plot, that's the second."

"But what about Mother?"

"That's an excellent question. And one I don't know the answer to yet. I must think."

ALL OVER THE CASTLE, in that hour, people were thinking.

Christian puzzled over his contraption. And over Marigold.

Marigold thought about Christian. And Olympia.

Ed worried about missing the LEFT Conference and never getting his best shot at a slice of the tooth fairy business. Or at the red-haired maiden. His recent dungeon experience had persuaded him that opportunities for good things should be grabbed and not postponed. You never knew when you wouldn't be around anymore. He'd never get anywhere if he just sat around cooling his thumbs.

Bub and Cate wondered what Christian was trying to get them to do.

Olympia changed clothes time after time and concentrated on keeping all her balls in the air: arranging the wedding, keeping Swithbert out of the way, deciding what method of extermination to use on Ed and Christian once they'd been convicted of treason, and being charming to her many guests.

Swithbert and Marigold sought a solution to the problems of Olympia and Magnus.

Marigold's sisters, Calista, Tatiana, and Eve, all worried about what they would wear to the wedding that would please their mother enough to keep her off their backs. Now that they had their own kingdoms and the power to arrange their lives to suit themselves, they recognized how little they wanted to be the kind of wife and mother that Olympia had been. Getting away from her had freed them to be smarter and more sensible than she'd ever given them credit for being. Mostly, she'd been interested in how they looked, which had always been spectacular, even though Olympia could invariably find some fault.

Oddly, since leaving home, they all seemed even more beautiful, in a ripe, fully realized way.

Rollo decided to take a troop of soldiers across the river to search the troll's cave for evidence they could use to seal the fate of Edric and his girlfriend-stealing pal.

Magnus tried to participate in all the festivities while wondering what it would be like to be married to someone he had so little in common with. Oh, it would be wonderful to have his own home, but what would they talk about? What would they do together? He'd never finished a book in his whole life, and she had at least one with her at all times. He loved to fish—maybe she did, too—and he loved drawing elegant maps that showed where the rivers and forests and dragons and sea serpents were; maybe he could interest her in that. But he was afraid of dogs and she had three. He knew he really was a shy and simple person, and Marigold was anything but. It just didn't seem as if it could possibly work for either of them— and that was even without considering Olympia, his terrifying mother-in-law-to-be.

The wedding guests thought only of the next meal, the next entertainment, the next amusement. They were there for a good time, weren't they?

17

Rollo and his soldiers ransacked the cave, not even stopping to admire the gorgeous light that filtered through the crystals. Walter and Carrie perched in a candleberry tree outside the cave and watched, their heads cocked quizzically.

The soldiers couldn't understand why there was so much stuff in the cave: piles of clothing and piles of tools, shelves of books and rows of boots, all carefully segregated by type. It was the racks of weapons that firmly convinced Rollo that an insurrection was under way. The boots and clothing and other things must belong to the insurrectionists—and from the looks of things, there were a lot of them.

"No clues as to where his army is hiding," Rollo said, "but we can prevent a tragedy by confiscating these weapons. Anybody find anything else suspicious?"

"This band sure has a lot of junk," a soldier said. "Lucky this cave has so many rooms to put it in. There's a whole room of left gloves!"

"Is there one of right gloves?" asked another soldier.

"Not that I've found yet. There's a chest full of forks and right next to it is a chest full of jewelry, as if forks and jewels were equal in value. I can't figure out the system."

"You think this is important?" a soldier asked Rollo, showing him the wickerwork hamper with the napkin-wrapped bundle in it. "Seems funny, just this one little thing in the hamper when every other container in the place is stuffed full."

Rollo unwrapped the napkin, revealing the little blue velvet suit. It had been untouched for so long that it had begun to split along the folds. As Rollo shook it out, a tiny tinkle made him look in one of the pockets. He held up the chain, still as golden and shiny as the day Ed had put it there, and examined the charm hanging from it.

"Holy buckets!" he said. "We've got to tell somebody about this! That troll is in a lot more trouble than we even knew. He's a murderer!"

CHRISTIAN PUTTERED over his contraption, adjusting this and that, moving the dogs around to different places inside of it, making them whine and cock their ears in puzzlement.

"Oh, quit looking like I'm doing something bad to you," he said to them. "You'll be heroes by the time I'm through."

Bub whimpered while Cate rolled her eyes and yelped dramatically.

OLYMPIA, WITH FENLEIGH crouched next to her, fussed over Swithbert's evening dosage. She didn't want to give him too much—he'd have to be alert enough in the morning to walk Marigold down the aisle. But she wanted to make sure he stayed well out of the way until then. She tapped a finger against her teeth and pondered.

A knock at her chamber door caused her to start, and then to throw a scarf over her table. "Enter!" she called.

Calista, Tatiana, and Eve came in, done up in their wedding finery. Olympia embraced them one by one and kissed the air beside their cheeks.

"My darlings!" she exclaimed. "How splendid you all look. There are no more beautiful daughters in all the world."

"Thank you, Mother," they said in unison, breathing a collective sigh of relief. Tatiana, the eldest of the triplets by three minutes and the one who had been given the fairy birth-gift of boldness, said, "We knew you'd want to see what we're wearing to the wedding." Under her breath, she muttered, "So we thought we'd get that ordeal over with."

"My angels!" Olympia exclaimed. "How could you look any better? Though, Tatiana, don't you have a tiara with a bigger diamond? Why don't you wear that one? Bigger is always better when it comes to diamonds, don't you think?"

Tatiana had always thought the bigger diamond was vulgar. She only wore that tiara in the privacy of her chambers when she was playing dress-up with her little daughter.

"Calista," Olympia went on, "are you sure you want to wear that color? Wouldn't the ashes-of-roses gown bring out your eyes better? What you have on makes you look a little, oh, sallow. Didn't you notice?"

Calista's huge blue eyes, which always looked marvelous no matter what she had on, narrowed with exasperation. She got more compliments on this gown than on any she owned. How was it that when she was growing up she'd thought her mother was always right? What a relief to know it wasn't so.

"And Eve," Olympia continued. "How pretty you'd look if your hair were just a bit more—oh, I don't know, *arranged*, I suppose. Do you know what I mean?"

Eve, whose birth-gift was gentleness, and who had always been the most intimidated by Olympia, didn't have the faintest idea what her mother meant. She and her abigail had spent a long giggly time that afternoon getting her hair into this arrangement, and they both thought it looked quite splendid.

"Would you like to see Marigold's wedding dress?" Olympia asked.

"Of course," they agreed, remembering the wedding-gown-in-triplicate they'd had to wear at their own triple wedding—the one their mother had designed in such an extravagant fashion that they had all felt overwhelmed, as if *it* were wearing *them*. But they had made a pact that they would wear whatever they had to in order to marry their royal sweethearts and get out into their own kingdoms and their own lives.

If anything, Marigold's gown was even worse than theirs had been. It was so rococo as to be grotesque, with no inch unembellished by a bow or an embroidered flower or an appliquéd something-or-other, or a brilliant, a seed pearl, or a bead.

The sisters exchanged appalled glances before Calista, the one whose birth-gift was practicality, asked, "How does Marigold look in it? She's so petite, she must be completely buried."

"Don't be ridiculous," Olympia said, at her most imperious. "She needs all the help she can get. She wanted a completely unadorned gown and a plain veil with her best everyday tiara. Can you imagine? Why, she'd look like a washerwoman."

"I think that sounds just right for her," Eve said softly.

The triplets agreed that Marigold had never been as plain as their mother insisted to everyone that she was. Marigold was just different from the rest of them, that's all—small and delicate, dark eyed and dark haired, with ivory skin, while the triplets were blond and tall and buxom, with pink cheeks and sapphire blue eyes.

"Oh, really, Eve," Olympia said. "What judgment you have. The way you and Calista will run Zandelphia when Beaufort breathes his last—well, I shudder to think."

Truth be known, Eve and Calista were shuddering

to think about it, too, since King Beaufort had recently been taken quite ill—so ill, in fact, that he hadn't been able to make it to the wedding. He was so awfully bossy and dyspeptic that they weren't sure they'd actually miss him if he were to go to his reward, but when he did, *they* were the next in line.

Calista and Eve and Princes Teddy and Harry had had many talks about how to be good monarchs, and they thought that they could probably pull it off most of the time. But they didn't really want to do it. Worrying over affairs of state and regal demeanor and stuff like that didn't appeal much to them. They would prefer to have someone else run Zandelphia while they continued doing what they best liked to do: play with their children, breed championship Norfolk terriers (of which the sale to neighboring kingdoms greatly benefited the Royal Treasury of Zandelphia), and arrange fairs for Zandelphia's subjects.

They quite admired the fact that Tatiana was already Queen of Middle Sanibar, had taken to it almost effortlessly, and was reigning spectacularly well—with very little help from King Willie. He was a dear, nobody could argue with that, but he was more interested in his horticultural experiments than in governing. Luckily, he was smart enough not to interfere with Tatiana's natural leadership talents. As a consequence Middle Sanibar was enjoying great peace and prosperity.

"I haven't seen Papa since we arrived," Calista said, dropping the fruitless discussion of Marigold's wedding dress. After all, wearing a dreadful dress for a few hours was a small price to pay for one's freedom. "Is he well?"

"Oh, your poor papa," Olympia said sadly. "He's failed quite a lot since you last saw him, I'm afraid. You must prepare to be shocked when you see him tomorrow."

"Tomorrow?" Tatiana said. "Why can't we see him now?"

"He's resting. He needs all his strength for the wedding. I must forbid it."

The triplets made silent vows to get in to see him that very day no matter what their mother said.

"And Marigold," Tatiana said, "we must see Marigold before the wedding."

"Tomorrow will be soon enough," Olympia said smoothly. "She's prostrate with nerves, poor dear."

The sisters looked at each other. Mother calling Marigold "poor dear"? Marigold, who was tough as an old boot when she needed to be, "prostrate with nerves"? Papa stashed away? What was up around here?

"I'm going to see her," Tatiana stated, sounding

like the queen she was. She had learned how easy it was for a queen to push people around just by the tone of her voice—she'd had her initial instruction from Olympia, hadn't she?—and, though she didn't do it often, she recognized that there were times when it was appropriate, and even necessary.

"Tomorrow," Olympia said definitively. She'd been a queen longer than Tatiana had, after all. "Now run along, girls, and change. I must change, too. Soon it will be time for the jugglers and the fire-eater and the trained bear to perform in the Great Hall."

"I don't know about you two," Tatiana said as they left their mother's apartments and headed down the hall, "but I want to see Papa and Marigold right now."

"Me, too," Eve said. "How come we let Mother get away with pushing us around so much when we were girls? Why were we so afraid of her?"

"Because she yelled and wouldn't speak to us, and when she did, she said mean things," Calista said. "It's what we call a tantrum when our children do it."

"But she did more than that," Tatiana went on. "Remember all the maids she banished? All the footmen she exiled? All the servants who've gone from dining hall duty to shoveling out the stables?"

"But we weren't maids or servants. We were her family," Eve said.

"I don't think she made a distinction," Calista said. "We were all supposed to do what she said."

"Apparently she still thinks that," Tatiana said.

The sisters stopped walking. The carpet they trod upon was handwoven in France and had taken twelve years to create. The walls were lined with gilt-framed portraits of generations of ancestors, back to Louis the Stammerer. On pedestals along the hall sat priceless porcelain vases and statues sculpted by master artists. And the sisters were thinking that it all amounted to a high-class prison, run by a beautiful and tyrannical warden.

"I wonder," Eve said slowly, "if Marigold really wants to marry Magnus?"

"Why do you wonder that?" Calista asked. "I've never met him, but he sounds all right."

"Has it occurred to you that now that we're married and gone, Mother has only to get rid of Marigold and Papa to have the throne all to herself? Doesn't that sound like something she'd want to do?"

"But Magnus has no kingdom of his own," Tatiana reminded her. "He and Marigold would stay here. If that was what she was thinking of, why wouldn't she find a prince or a king who lived far away?"

"She's tried," Eve said. "Marigold hasn't cooperated. Magnus is the bottom of the barrel."

"But why would Marigold marry Magnus—I swear, saying that makes my lips vibrate—if she didn't want to?" Calista asked. "She doesn't have to marry at all to inherit. And you know Marigold has never been crazy about marriage, considering the one she grew up watching."

"We watched the same one, and we have happy marriages," Eve reminded her.

"We've been very lucky, too," Tatiana responded.

They were silently grateful for a moment until Tatiana said, "She'd do it to please Papa. If she thought Papa was...you know, on his way out...and he wanted to see her married before he...you know... she might. Papa's the only one she's ever wanted to please."

"We *really* need to talk to Marigold," Calista said.

"Now!" Tatiana agreed.

The sisters grabbed hands and, three abreast, ran down the exquisitely carpeted hallway to Marigold's suite.

18

It was empty. Pristine and empty. No nervous, prostrate bride-to-be in the great canopy bed. No flurry of maids preparing the trousseau. No piles of gifts and flowers from the eager bridegroom.

"You don't think Mother's done something to Marigold, do you?" Eve asked, her voice trembling.

"I wouldn't put it past her," Tatiana said, her eyes narrowing. "But she wouldn't do it until after the wedding. She wouldn't want to be cheated out of that spectacle. We've got to find Papa!"

Holding hands again, the sisters ran up a wide curving staircase, down a hall, around two corners, and up a narrow flight of steps to their father's unique set of rooms in the northwest turret. The door was locked from the inside.

"Papa!" Tatiana called, banging on the door. "Are you in there? It's us—Tatiana and Eve and Calista. We need to talk to you."

Denby's voice came through the door. "Is the queen with you?"

"No. It's her we need to talk to you about."

There was a long silence. Tatiana pounded again. "Papa! We're plotting a mutiny! We need your help."

Their papa opened the door looking quite chipper and lively, his cheeks pink and his eyes bright. "My dears," he said, embracing each of them briefly and formally.

"Is that your nightshirt tucked into your breeches, Papa?" Calista asked, wondering if, though he looked perfectly healthy, his mind was off its hinges.

"Oh," Swithbert said, looking down at himself. "I guess it is. Denby, would you fetch me a shirt, please? From the *dressing room*?"

Something about the way he emphasized the words made the triplets take notice. They might be blonds, but there was nothing dumb about them. What was going on in the dressing room that their papa wanted to keep secret?

Denby opened the dressing room door just enough

to squeeze through and shut it quickly. The sisters raised their eyebrows at one another.

"Are you all right, Papa?" Eve asked. "Mother said you were doing poorly."

"I'm fit as a violin," he said, sitting on his auxiliary throne next to a diamond-paned window that overlooked the flagstone terrace. "Now, what's this about a mutiny?"

So the sisters laid out their half-formed fears about Marigold and Magnus's marriage, tiptoeing around their suspicions that their mother might be involved somehow in something disagreeable—or actually nefarious, if you got right down to it.

When they were finished, their father said, "I had no idea that, because of your mother, you were such unhappy children. You seemed so content."

"We weren't defiant, the way Marigold is," Tatiana said, "but we had one another to commiserate with."

"Besides," Calista said, "the best way to avoid Mother's wrath was to act cooperative. We saw what happened to Marigold. All those evenings in her room without supper—"

"I always smuggled her something on a tray," Swithbert said.

"—and all that time spent picking out the stitches on other people's botched embroidery as punishment for some minor thing, and all those awful gowns poor Marigold had to wear, even worse than the three-just-alike ones we had to wear. We see now that we should have protected our little sister more, but we were just kids ourselves then."

"Now we have another chance to do that," Tatiana said.

"Because Mother's getting out of control," Calista added. "It's time somebody stopped her."

Eve, who had been silent until then, asked, "Why did you let her get away with so much, Papa?"

He shook his head sadly. "I'd never known anyone like her. I'd grown up with quiet, gentle people, and when our marriage was arranged, I'd never even met Olympia. I admit she dazzled me at first, so beautiful and fiery and headstrong—and so completely unfamiliar. I was a lot older than she was. I guess I was too indulgent—more like a doting parent than a husband. I gave her too much latitude, I see it now, but I didn't know how to stop her. You girls are right, though. I know exactly what she's planning, and it's time to bring a halt to her tactics. Now."

Eve's voice was tender with understanding and forgiveness. "Papa. Where's Marigold? Do you know?"

"I do."

"Is she safe?"

"She is now," Swithbert said grimly. "And I'm going to keep her that way." How odd it was that at this moment of desperate crisis, he felt more alive than he had in years.

"Can we see her?" Tatiana asked. "I think it's time we explained a few things about the kind of big sisters we were."

"And try to make it up to her," Calista added.

Swithbert went to the dressing room door and opened it. "Marigold, precious. Your sisters want to talk to you," he said.

It took them so long to sort out everything that was going on, as well as their long history of misunderstandings, that they completely forgot about Olympia bringing the evening drink for Swithbert. When she pounded on the door, they jumped as if they'd been struck by lightning.

"Quick, girls," Swithbert said. "Get in the dressing room!" He hopped into bed, pulling the covers up to his chin. Fortunately, he'd gotten so involved in his conversation with his daughters that he'd never put on the fresh shirt Denby had brought him, and was still in his nightshirt. "Okay, Denby," he said when the girls were safely stashed away. "Let her in."

"What's the meaning of this?" Olympia demanded, her face a storm cloud. "Where's my maid? Why did it take you so long to answer the door? And why was it locked?"

"My fault, Your Majesty," Denby said humbly, bowing from the waist, his hands clasped. "I dismissed Millie because the king wasn't doing anything but sleeping. I know every hand is needed to help, what with all the extra guests in the castle. I can watch over him as well as she, and I had nothing else to do. I locked the door to protect his privacy. I didn't think you'd want any wedding guests stumbling in here and seeing him like that. I must have dozed off, too. It's not the most stimulating thing, watching someone else sleep."

"If you're going to watch him, then I want you to *watch* him. Now, prop him up so I can give him his nighttime draught. I must get on to my guests for the evening entertainment."

Denby held Swithbert up by the shoulders. Olympia took the cork from the bottle and held it to the king's lips. As she poured, his head lolled limply, and the gray liquid trickled from the corner of his mouth.

"Blast!" she exclaimed. "He's too far gone to swallow *again*! All right, it'll be your job to get it down him once he wakes up, just like you did yesterday and the day before. You know what will happen to you if you forget."

"Of course, Your Majesty. Don't give it another thought." Denby bowed deeply.

Olympia cast a look around the room. "That frankincense tree isn't looking too well," she said. "I'll have someone come up to replace it." Her eyes swept the room again. She hesitated for a moment, then she picked up her skirts and made for the door. "Don't forget the dose, Denby—or you'll be very sorry."

As soon as the door closed behind her, Denby turned the key in the lock and whispered, "She's gone."

Swithbert popped up and the door to the dressing room opened.

"Don't drink that, Papa," Marigold said, spotting the bottle Olympia had left on the bedside table.

"Don't worry," Swithbert said. "I haven't had any in a couple of days. Look what it's done to the frankincense tree." The poor tree shuddered, and a few more leaves fell.

"Now, the first thing we have to do is hide Marigold very well, until after the wedding has been called off," Swithbert continued. "Then we find Magnus and make it up to him somehow. I've always been fond of the boy, and this will be a big disappointment for him."

"Let's get Chris and Ed and the dogs out of the

dungeon before we take care of Magnus," Marigold reminded her father.

"We'll get around to that, my dear, when the time is right," he said, patting her hand. "Don't worry. Denby, take a look out there. Go all the way down the steps and check the hall to make sure the coast is clear before we move Marigold."

Denby went to the door but couldn't open it. He twiddled with the key in the lock, but the lock held fast. "It feels as if it's barred from the outside," he said.

Alarmed, Swithbert hustled into the dressing room and tried the back door out of his suite. It, too, was barred from the outside.

"We're locked in," Swithbert said. "It has to be Olympia's doing. How in the world—" His eyes fell on the table where he and his daughters had sat, drinking tea and winkling out the whole story of Olympia's treachery. When they had scattered, running from Olympia's knock, they had forgotten about Calista's tiara, Tatiana's scarf, and the sash to Marigold's dressing gown, all left untidily on the chairs. Olympia hadn't missed a thing. She knew they were all there, and now they weren't leaving.

"Curses!" Swithbert exclaimed. "You can't stage a mutiny in slow motion; we took too long getting organized!"

They spent the rest of the night pacing, cursing, and trying without success to devise a solution.

CHRISTIAN SPENT THE NIGHT perfecting his creation. After a while Ed got interested enough to help him. He decided that, by hook or by ladder, he'd do anything to get himself out of incarceration in time for the LEFT Conference. After a reluctant start, Bub and Cate had thrown themselves wholeheartedly into the project and were having the time of their lives. Whether it worked or not was beside the point to them, as is usual with dogs.

19

Olympia partied. She kissed her guests—some of them more thoroughly than others—and drank some wine and danced with Magnus and tried to figure out what to do about her rebellious family. When King Willie and Princes Teddy and Harry came to her asking where Tatiana, Calista, and Eve were, she shrugged prettily and said they were probably off somewhere catching up on sisterly gossip.

All she knew for sure was that in just one day, Marigold was going to marry Magnus. *Nobody* was going to make this queen look like a fool in front of most of the royalty in the known world.

At dawn Olympia came with a troop of her soldiers to Swithbert's suite. Banging on the door, she called, "Don't bother to prevaricate. I know you're all in there. I want Marigold. It's time for her to get ready for the wedding. If she doesn't come out, there's going to be a terrible tragedy that will wipe out my whole family in one swoop. I'll be an elegant, grief-stricken queen, don't you think? So brave, so resolute, with the kingdom to rule all by myself."

She could hear frantic whispering inside, and stood her ground confidently. Marigold had no choice but to come out. She wasn't going to sacrifice her father and her sisters just because Magnus wasn't to her taste. Olympia knew it.

And, of course, Marigold did. What else could she do? If she hadn't come out, she'd have signed all of their death warrants. By marrying Magnus she was signing only her own. And marrying him bought time—with time, maybe they could still find a way around Olympia's wicked plans. She'd just made three new friends—her sisters—and she wasn't willing to let them go so easily or so soon.

She stood like a big doll while the abigails, under Olympia's instructions, dressed her and did her hair and sprayed her with perfume. Her mind was in her father's suite with him and her sisters, and in the dungeon with Christian and Ed and the dogs. She didn't even know where Flopsy, Mopsy, and Topsy were. Olympia told her that they were just fine—and would stay that way as long as Marigold did as she was told. Fenleigh sprawled luxuriously on the chaise, safe for once from the yaps and nips and chasings of Marigold's three little mops.

In Swithbert's chamber Denby, under guard, was preparing the king for the wedding ceremony. The triplets had been removed to an adjoining suite to be prepared also. They all felt more as if they were dressing for a funeral. Which indeed they were, even if it would be some time in the future.

IN THE DUNGEON Christian was saying, "I think we're ready. First the door."

Among the blacksmith's discards he'd found a small tin of what he suspected—and hoped—was Inflamium. He packed some around the hinges of the cell door. Then he struck a piece of metal against the wall of the cell until he got a spark, which fell into a pile of dog fur he'd collected from Bub and Cate. Cate had thrown a fit of miffed vanity when she'd seen the bald spot the fur-harvesting had left on her leg. But now that she saw what a merry little fire her fur made, she was pleased with her contribution to the escape attempt and swaggered importantly around the dungeon.

The fur fire ignited a slim stick of wood from the junk pile, which Chris touched to the stuff packed around the hinges. The flame sputtered for a moment, then went out.

"Rats," Christian said. "I'll have to try it again. Line up, Bub and Cate. I need more fur."

Cate was even less cooperative this time. She could envision herself being denuded for the sake of an experiment that never worked. But between them, Ed and Christian managed to hold her down long enough to get what they needed. In truth, Chris knew he could have gotten all the fur he needed from shaggy, cooperative Bub. But he also knew that, if the experiment succeeded, Cate would never forgive him for not letting her contribute to what would in time, in her own mind, be her single-pawed role in the saving of all of their skins—if they were lucky.

Christian went through the routine again. This time when the ignited stuff began to sputter, he blew on the tiny embers, coaxing them into steady burning.

"Step back, everyone," he said once he was sure the fire wasn't going out. "Turn your backs." He had to lift Cate bodily and turn her from the door.

They waited.

And waited. "No peeking," Christian warned, crossing all his fingers and praying that what he'd found really was Inflamium.

Just when he was about to acknowledge that it wasn't, there was a pop and then a *boom!* and the cell door blew out into the corridor.

"Wow!" Ed said.

Cate and Bub dashed out of the cell, barking excitedly.

"Quiet!" Christian hollered after them, and then lowered his voice. "Quiet," he whispered. "We have to be very sneaky now."

"Hey!" called the guard from the next cell. "Let me out, too."

"I don't think so," Christian said. "We don't want anybody running upstairs and blowing the whistle on us. Where are the keys to the dungeon doors?"

"Why should I tell you?" the guard pouted, turning his back. The effect was somewhat spoiled by the fact that his breeches hung down a little too far in the rear.

"Think!" Christian implored Ed. "We've got to get out of here and stop that wedding. Something's gone wrong. I know it, or Marigold and the king would have been here long ago to let us out. Where would the keys be?"

Without a word, Ed pointed to a hook on the wall

by the door. There hung a ring with many keys on it, right where Swithbert had tidily left it.

"Oh," Christian said, snatching the key ring and beginning to try keys in the big lock. Once, he dropped the ring and couldn't remember which keys he'd already tried, so he had to start all over. "Rats!" he muttered. "Rats, mice, and rodents!"

The last key on the ring was the one that finally turned in the lock.

"Hooray!" he said. "Now let's get the machine."

They wheeled out of the cell the cumbersome machine Christian had constructed, at one point having to turn it on its side to get it to fit through the doorway.

Dragging it up the steps to the dungeon doors was an even trickier maneuver. Christian was torn between the need to hurry and the need to go slowly enough not to damage the machine.

While they labored, the imprisoned guard wheedled, "Aw, come on, get me out of here. I can help you. I'm strong. I can get that thing up the stairs. What are you going to do with it, anyway? Looks like something put together by a blindfolded committee."

That did it.

Christian, who was very proud of this contraption whether it worked or not, wouldn't let that guard out now if the building were on fire. Well, okay, if the building were on fire. But only then.

Ed was only minimally more helpful than the dogs, so Christian did most of the heavy lifting himself, finally muscling the thing into the wide corridor outside the dungeon. The corridor was empty, lit with burning torches in wall sconces.

"Nobody's around," Christian said. "They're not expecting any trouble from here. They must all be up at the wedding. We've got to find a way to the outdoors without being noticed."

"Who'd notice a caravan like us—two dogs, a strange machine, and a troll?"

"What about me, the mad scientist?" Christian asked.

"All right, a mad scientist, too," Ed added. "Who'd notice that?"

"Nobody, I hope," Christian said, pushing his machine down the hall.

20

Marigold, in her overloaded wedding gown, stood back from the arched entrance to the flagstone terrace, her hand on her father's arm. The wedding guests were seated on the terrace in little gilt chairs, dressed in their dazzling finest, waiting. Calista, Eve, and Tatiana, Marigold's attendants, had already gone down to the altar, which was set up at one end of the terrace under a bower of summer flowers. They stood looking back toward the archway, their expressions anything but joyful. Magnus, on the other side of the altar, exhibited a remarkably similar expression and was unable to keep his knees from knocking rapidly together.

The chamber orchestra played on and on, and the

guests began to shift in their seats. Where was the bride? This was the main event, and they were anxious for it to begin, to see if the wedding lived up to the lavish, no-holds-barred celebrating of the past couple of days. If they noticed how glum the bridesmaids looked or how agitated the bridegroom was, they put it down to wedding jitters.

Marigold and Swithbert would have stood there in the archway indefinitely if Olympia, carrying Fenleigh under her arm as always, hadn't come up behind them and said, "We're starting a new tradition. *Both* parents are walking the bride down the aisle. Let's go."

She took Marigold's other arm and practically dragged her and the king out onto the terrace. The music flared and the guests stood, craning for a look at this unprecedented arrangement.

Olympia smiled and nodded as she went down the aisle, singling out especially influential personages for her notice. You never knew when you might need a favor, and believe it or not, people remembered even such apparently trivial things as a special nod.

Marigold and Swithbert weren't smiling or nodding at anybody. They were moving like mechanical toys, stiff and expressionless. Marigold's mind whirled with anxiety. She could think of no other solution but to throw herself over the parapet and down into the river, and she knew she could never do that. Not only would it break her father's heart, it would leave him at the queen's mercy. If going through with this wedding meant being shackled to Magnus for a lifetime—even a very short one—she knew she had to do it to protect her papa.

Swithbert was feeling like a failure. How had he allowed things to come to such a pass? He thought he'd been a decent king, but apparently he'd only been a weak one. Without his even noticing, Olympia had taken over, getting rid of most of the old familiar retainers at the castle; managing their daughters' lives; turning his soldiers suspicious and paranoid, ready for a fight when there was no good reason for one. Now he couldn't even protect his beloved Marigold from this tangled situation he'd allowed to come about.

But wait. Maybe he could! When it came time for him to answer the question, "Who gives this woman in marriage?" he could say he wouldn't. Then he sighed. Olympia would be standing right beside him. She'd say he wasn't of sound mind, everyone knew that, and, of course, they *both* gave up Marigold to Magnus, so proceed with the ceremony, please.

The opulently robed bishop beamed and began to intone the solemn and frightening words of the wedding ceremony: "in sickness and in health . . . until death do you part." Swithbert had never noticed how many ominous words were in the marriage vows—*sickness*, *death*, *put asunder.*

Suddenly Swithbert heard murmuring behind him, spreading like a wave, becoming louder and louder until it was pierced by a scream and the sound of little gilt chairs toppling over. He turned and saw the wedding guests stampeding out of the way of . . . of . . . what the heck was that, anyway? It looked like a giant dragonfly, with wings that flapped ponderously up and down, sometimes more quickly than at other times. It weaved, dipping and rising at the edge of the parapet, disappearing below the rim and then coming into view again, seeming to struggle to make it over the terrace wall.

The next time it rose, Swithbert could see that it wasn't a real bug—it was mechanical. Powered by—could it be . . . dogs?—running on a kind of treadmill belt in the center. When the dogs slowed, the flying machine dipped; when they ran faster, it rose. Behind him he heard Marigold cry, "Christian!"

And Christian yelled back, "You said the only way you could get out of here is if you had wings! I've come to get you and take you away!"

And overlapping Chris's voice was Olympia's yelling, "Get me Rollo! And all his archers! And hurry up!"

The wedding guests were panicking, trying to escape by squeezing through the arched doorway to the staircase, pushing and shoving and stepping on each other's ermine-trimmed capes and trailing trains in a most unroyal way.

As the guests rushed down, Rollo and his soldiers were running *up* the stairs, trying to reach the terrace. The collision was a terrible mess, but as usual, the group with the weapons won. The soldiers raced out onto the terrace, leaving behind them a trail of upended royalty sprawled on the stairs and on each other.

Among all the fairies in attendance, only Queen Mab, with her lousy sense of direction, didn't make it down the staircase but remained flitting haphazardly from here to there around the terrace.

"Shoot that...that...thing!" Olympia commanded, as the flying machine edged up over the parapet again. The archers quickly arranged themselves in two ranks, one standing and one kneeling, while Rollo bellowed at them.

The flying machine sank again and then, with one strong burst, came heaving over the wall just as the archers let their arrows fly. Arrows bounced off some parts of the machine and pierced others as it crash-landed onto the flagstones.

The dogs jumped off the treadmill and ran yapping hysterically (Hecate) and baying bravely (Beelze-bub) straight at the soldiers. Ed untangled himself from the wreckage and ran, too, but in the other direction, down the whole long length of the terrace.

"Get him!" Rollo screamed. "He's a murderer!"

Several soldiers took off after him, two of them hindered by dogs attached to their pants legs. Even so handicapped, a young long-legged soldier could outrun an old short-legged troll any day of the week, and so they did.

While the soldiers grappled with Ed and the dogs, Christian was lying in the crumpled remains of the flying machine—an arrow protruding from the center of his chest.

Marigold screamed and ran for the wreck, stopping only to throw off her heavy crown and veil, and to rip off the voluminous train of her ridiculous wedding gown.

"Christian!" she cried, climbing over the broken flying machine. She slid to her knees and took his head into her lap. "Speak to me," she pleaded. "Tell me you're all right."

He moaned but didn't open his eyes.

"Papa!" she called. "Help me!"

"Stay right where you are, Swithbert," Olympia ordered.

"Or what?" he asked her. "I'm the king, in case you've forgotten. And it's high time I started acting like it."

"Well!" Olympia said huffily, and stalked away.

"Denby! Go for the castle doctor," the king ordered.

"I believe he's at the foot of the stairs, tending to all the people who fell down them on the rush to get out of here."

"Well, go get him anyway. I'm the king. He has to do what I say."

With that, Denby headed off and the king made for the pile of broken parts that contained his daughter and Christian.

Nobody paid the slightest attention to Calista, Eve, and Tatiana except for their husbands, who had rushed up in the midst of all the commotion exclaiming, "Where have you *been*?"

"Oh, Papa," Marigold cried when Swithbert reached her. "Do you think he'll be all right?"

"I'm sure he will," Swithbert reassured her, although he wasn't sure at all. An arrow in your chest didn't seem like a very hopeful sign.

"Did you see, Papa?" Marigold asked, her eyes shining. "He was flying! He was coming to fly me away! Don't you think that's amazing? Don't you think that's wonderful?"

Swithbert waited for a moment before he asked the next question, afraid of the answer. "And why do you think he did that, precious? Why did he go to so much trouble and endanger himself so much? I know *I* wouldn't want to travel in anything that depended upon dogs for its locomotion."

Marigold didn't even need to answer. Her cheeks pinked prettily, making her look like the blushing bride she evidently wasn't going to be.

Christian groaned again just as Denby returned with the doctor.

"Step back, everyone," the doctor said, carrying his bag full of leeches, bloodletting tools, and trepanning instruments. "Let me have a look at him."

Marigold didn't move. "You can look at him just fine while I stay here." She held Christian's head firmly in her lap with both hands.

The doctor shrugged and then knelt, while Swithbert removed himself. Under the bridal arbor stood Olympia and Magnus. Swithbert heard Magnus ask, "Does this mean the wedding is off?"

"Must you act like such an idiot, Magnus?" Olympia said, and strode away to have a look at Ed, pinned down by several soldiers. The dogs scampered around the group, snapping and growling and eluding the detail that Rollo had assigned to capture them.

"What's this about a murderer?" Olympia asked sternly. "Don't we have enough problems without that, too?"

Fenleigh took one look at Bub and crawled up onto Olympia's shoulder, as far away as he could get from that mouthful of big teeth.

"But this troll *is* a murderer, Your Majesty," Rollo said. "Remember, years back, when Prince Teddy and Prince Harry's older brother was lost in the forest and never seen again? And everybody decided he'd been eaten by wild animals because no body was ever found? Well, I discovered the boy's clothes in a basket in the troll's cave. He must have done the kid in. The clothes are old and musty, but there are no animal teeth marks on them."

"And how do you know those are the little prince's clothes?"

"Because of the pendant I found in the pocket of his suit. It's a golden phoenix. Everybody knows only the royalty of the kingdom of Zandelphia are allowed to wear that emblem."

"I didn't kill anybody!" Ed bellowed.

Olympia leaned over him, with Swithbert behind her. "Then what about that blue velvet suit?" she asked. "And the phoenix charm?"

"Phoenix, schmoenix—what do I know about phoenixes? Is that what it is? I thought it was just a weird-looking bird. And the suit's his, too; he said he never wanted to wear either one of them things again."

"Who? Who said that?" Olympia demanded.

"Well, *Christian*. Who else?" Ed said. "I found him in the forest when he was just a little boy. I wanted to send him home, but he said he didn't want to go. He said he'd tell everybody I kidnapped him if I tried to make him leave. So, well, he just stayed."

"Why, you're right," Queen Mab, who was still flitting around, put in. "I knew he seemed familiar when I first met him with you in the forest, but I never expected to see Prince Christian with a pushy old troll, so I didn't make the connection."

"Why am I not surprised," Ed muttered.

There was a stunned silence while Swithbert and Olympia absorbed this information. If what Ed and Mab said was true, Christian was the rightful heir to the crown of Zandelphia. Which meant that Olympia had had a future king and his guardian thrown in her dungeon and scheduled for execution. It also meant, she realized, that Calista and Eve would not be queens of Zandelphia, something Olympia had been counting on to enhance her reputation: She intended to be known as the mother of three queens.

Of course, they could still become queens if Christian didn't survive.

21

Swithbert was thinking, Well, how do you like that? Marigold could get to be queen of Zandelphia. Then she and two of her sisters could all be in the same kingdom.

Olympia turned back to look at the doctor. He had one foot on Christian's shoulder for leverage while he got ready to yank the arrow from his chest.

"Wait!" she called, and hurried over, neglecting to notice how Marigold was watching her through narrowed, suspicious eyes. "Do you think it's a good idea to take that arrow out?"

The doctor looked at her, astonished. "It's the customary procedure," he said. "Most patients prefer to have their arrows removed rather than left in. Since he's unconscious, we can't ask him. So I'm using my best judgment."

"But won't removing it cause a lot of blood loss?" Olympia asked. "Why don't we leave it in for a while and see if he feels better?"

"The archers' arrows are often poisoned, Your Highness," the doctor reminded her.

"Yes, yes," she said impatiently, waving her hand. "But we don't know that *this* one is."

Swithbert, no dummy no matter what Olympia thought, knew exactly what was in her mind. "Hey!" he said, running to the wreck. "Get that arrow out *now!*"

The doctor, still gripping the arrow, involuntarily jerked on it at Swithbert's shout.

"Ooh," Christian moaned, coming closer to consciousness.

"Chris!" Ed called from the other end of the terrace. "Are you all right?"

Bub and Cate, torn between protecting Ed, escaping from the soldiers, going after Fenleigh, and checking up on Christian, ran around indecisively, as though they were demented.

"Those dogs are mad!" Rollo yelled. "They must be exterminated! Catch them!"

A few wedding guests began to creep back onto

the terrace to see what was going on, and found a five-ring circus: Calista, Eve, and Tatiana trying to explain to their baffled husbands what was happening; Ed held down on the ground by soldiers; the dogs going nuts; the crashed vehicle with Christian, Marigold, and the doctor amidst the wreckage; and Olympia and Swithbert arguing at the top of their lungs, hearts, and cerebellums about removing Christian's arrow. Magnus stood apart from everyone, looking bewildered and anxious.

While all this was going on, Marigold said quietly to the doctor, "Take that arrow out or I'll have you banished to Isobaria, where you'll do nothing but put poultices on sunburns and wipe runny noses. Do it now."

And the doctor did.

Christian cried out, a sound of such agony that for a moment, all the commotion stopped.

Marigold, holding him and as unhappy as she had ever been in her life, was able to feel through all her senses the pain that filled Christian, and she cried out, too.

Everyone who heard that double cry, without knowing they were going to do so, began to weep from the pure human empathy it made them feel. Everyone but Olympia.

"I must go change clothes," she said. "And so must

the groom. This wedding *will* go on." She grabbed Magnus, and they swept down the stairs. No one paid any attention.

In her anguish Marigold pressed her hands against Christian's ruined chest to still the pain, to stanch the blood flow, to bring him comfort. Her hands seemed very warm and to have a slight vibration in them, which spread up her arms and into the whole of her body. The harder she pressed on the wound, the warmer she became and the more her own pain diminished. So she continued to press.

The wedding guests around them began to wipe their tears with their trains, the hems of their ermine-trimmed robes, or their sleeves. Royals never carried their own handkerchiefs—someone else always handed them one when they needed it. Even the most powerful person can be dumb about simple things.

The doctor blew his nose on the wad of gauze he'd had ready to slap onto the great hole in Christian's chest.

"Let go of him, honey," he said gently to Marigold, for whom he felt a newly born affection. "I need to dress that wound." Marigold lifted her hands, which no longer felt so warm or so tingly, and wiped the blood onto the underskirt of her awful wedding gown.

The doctor mopped at the blood on Christian's chest with a fresh piece of gauze and then exclaimed, "I don't believe it!"

"What?" Marigold asked as she gazed at Christian's face. His eyes were still closed, but his features were no longer drawn with pain.

"Look."

Swithbert and several of the crowd around them leaned in to look, too.

Except for some streaks of blood left over from the doctor's untidy mopping, Christian's chest was unblemished. There was no sign of the hole the arrow had made, no scar, no nothing. His skin was as smooth and as tanned as it had always been.

"I'm going to have to write this up for the next *Medical Association Journal*," the doctor said. "There's a faction that says laughter is the best medicine, and a smaller one that says love is. I think I have some empirical evidence that..."

But by now no one was listening.

"Get that boy out of there," Swithbert ordered. "Take him down to the Green Suite. Get him some clean clothes. And some broth and bread and pudding. Put a guard on him. Nobody goes near him except me."

"And me!" Marigold said, climbing out of the wreckage.

"And me!" Ed called from under the pile of soldiers still pinning him down.

Bub and Cate barked a lot, meaning "And me!" too.

"Bring that troll to my quarters," Swithbert told the soldiers. "I want to talk to him." He looked around. "Where's the queen?" he asked.

"I think she went to change clothes," someone said.

"That could take forever," the king muttered. "Especially if she decides to bathe that weasel of hers. Or whatever it is."

Marigold went with Christian to the Green Suite. Swithbert and Ed—and the dogs, who wouldn't be separated from Ed—went to Swithbert's chambers. The wedding guests went to the Great Hall, where the reception was being moved, now that the terrace was such a mess. Even if there hadn't been a wedding, there was still feasting—what else to do with all that food so many people had labored over for so long? The guests didn't mind. The reception part was always more fun than the wedding part anyway. And as the guests mingled and talked about the extraordinary events of the morning, the gossip traveled throughout the castle, from royalty to servants to serfs and back again. Buzz, buzz, buzz.

"I always knew Queen Olympia was a bad one. She treated those girls of hers like dirt. Even the triplets, and everyone knew they were her favorites."

"That Sir Magnus is a pretty thing, isn't he? But dumb as a box of rocks, don't you think?"

"I knew Christian was a prince when first I laid me eyes on him. And when he built that new butter churn for me—well, that just proved it, didn't it? Just shows you what splendid taste I have in men, it does."

"We always knew Princess Marigold had powers, the way she can read minds when she touches you, but *this*—do you think she's a witch?"

"I hear she even looks different now. Not so plain and dowdy. Must be hard having those Valkyries for sisters."

"Have you seen the king? He's got a spring in his step I haven't seen in a very long time. There was a while there I thought he was a goner."

"Do you think there'll still be a wedding today?"

"Olympia said there would be. And she's changing clothes for it, so I'd count on it."

MARIGOLD SAT at Christian's bedside, his right hand in both of hers, waiting for him to wake up. She'd taken a few minutes to strip off her hideous destroyed wedding gown and throw on a simple frock of pale pink linen before she'd run to the Green Suite to be with him, but her hair still tumbled down her back and she was barefoot.

Bub and Cate, quite at home in the castle now, scampered between the king's turret and the Green Suite, guarding their scattered family. Marigold's three little floor mops had been released from their confinement and joined in all the racing up and down stairs, skidding around corners and whizzing through the legs of anyone in the way. Five dogs torpedo-ing around the corridors created quite a navigational hazard.

All the dogs were on Christian's bed when he opened his eyes. They hunched around him, their heads and ears cocked, their eyes warm and wet with concern.

"How odd," he said. "I never imagined angels would look like this."

"They're not angels," Marigold said, scared to death that the crash had damaged his brain.

He turned toward her. "Of course," he said. "I see that now. They're dogs. *You're* the angel."

"Oh, Christian," she said, leaning over him. "What makes you think I'm an angel?"

"Well, I'm dead, aren't I? And you're so beautiful. Do you have wings? Can I see them? I tried to make some for a flying machine, but they didn't work quite as well as I wanted them to."

"But you're not dead. Not at all. You're fine."

"Fine? How can I be fine? I remember the flying machine crashing, and the arrows—" He put his hand on his chest. Puzzled, he rubbed the place where the arrow had been, then pushed himself up in bed. The dogs closed in around him, watching as he unbuttoned the nightshirt the doctor had dressed him in. He looked down at himself. "I could have sworn—" he murmured.

"Oh, you had an arrow in you, all right," Marigold told him. "The doctor pulled it out."

"But... there's no mark. No scar. No nothing. I *must* be dead."

"No," she said. And she told him what had happened, how she had somehow healed his wound.

"I don't understand it," Christian said, taking her hands in both of his over the backs of Flopsy, Mopsy, Topsy, Bub, and Cate. "Do you?"

"Not entirely," she said, though she, too, was now a believer in the doctor's second theory of what constituted the best medicine. "There's something else. Ever since I did ... whatever I did ... I've lost my curse. I can't tell what anybody's thinking anymore. And I know I was unhappy enough to sense their thoughts because I wasn't sure you were going to be all right. I've touched you and Papa and one of the maids and the doctor, and it's gone. Whatever it was—some kind of power or energy or magic—it's used up. On you. There's a part of me in you now. That must have been the way to break the curse of my birth-gift, the way I had to find for myself. And I never would have without you."

The tear that Christian had felt in the corner of his heart seemed to knit itself up a little. "So you *are* an angel," he said. "*My* angel." And they looked at each other over the dogs as if there were no one else in all the world.

22

While all this was going on, Ed and the king were having a long talk over a very fine bottle of wine, one just a trifle insolent, with admirable flinty notes and a balanced fine-grained finish containing a wee hint of tumbleweed.

"So, Bert," Ed said, holding out his empty tankard again, "do you think there's anything you can do about this monopoly Mab's got going? Any help you can give me?"

"Sounds to me like you're doing just fine by yourself," Swithbert said, refilling both their tankards. "But I'd be glad to write a letter for you to add to the ones you've already got. And I'll get Teddy and Harry and

Willie to write letters, too. Can't hurt to have all us crowned heads in your corner."

Ed snapped his fingers. "I'll get *Christian* to write me a letter! He's got a pretty good crowned head of his own all of a sudden."

"How about that?" Swithbert said. "You know, I've been thinking—we've got wedding guests, a wedding reception, a wedding cake, bridesmaids, wedding gifts, and a bride. What's missing?"

Ed took a wild guess. "A groom?"

"A groom we've got. And I don't mean Magnus."

"Oh!" Ed said as he understood. "Well, I guess all we have to do is prop that arbor thing up again and get the bishop away from the roast pig and the ladies-in-waiting. All we're missing now is a wedding."

"So what are we waiting for?" Swithbert asked, swigging down the last of his wine. "Let's get going."

MARIGOLD AND CHRISTIAN were still gazing at each other across the dogs, who had finally collapsed from all the excitement and were piled up, snoring away, when Calista, Eve, and Tatiana came bursting into the room.

Tatiana took queenly control. "Come on, you two. You've got to get dressed."

"I'm not leaving Chris," Marigold said.

"Just for a few minutes," Tatiana said. "Then you can have him back."

"But why?" Marigold asked. "I'm dressed enough."

"You at least need shoes and a veil," Eve said.

"And Christian needs to brush his hair," Calista said, and stuck her hand out to him. "Hi. I'm Calista. Your brother Teddy's wife. And this is Eve, your brother Harry's wife. And Tatiana, Queen of Middle Sanibar, married to King Willie. We'll be your new sisters-in-law."

"Sisters-in-law?" Christian said, looking from Calista, Eve, and Tatiana to Marigold and back again in complete bewilderment. "My brothers?"

"Hasn't anybody told you?" Calista asked. "Now that you're the crown prince, heir to the throne of Zandelphia, you're husband material for Marigold, and the wedding's going to go on with you instead of Magnus as the groom."

"I'm the what?" Christian asked. Some of his hazy old memories surfaced a bit. Could those babies in the blue baskets have been Teddy and Harry? Could the long flight of stone steps and the little girl chasing the puppy have been in the castle at Zandelphia?

Marigold stood abruptly, furious tears pooling in her eyes. "Whose idea is this?" she demanded. "In the first place, I don't care if Christian *is* royalty; I'd marry him if he were a goatherd. And in the second place, he hasn't asked me. And in the third place, I'll not have him railroaded into something he doesn't want to do. Where's Mother? I'll tell her myself that there's going to be no wedding today."

"But I want one," Christian said, trying to get out from under the pile of dogs. "The only thing I want in all the world is for you to be my wife. We can sort out the rest of the stuff later."

"Oh," Marigold said.

Her sisters grabbed her and dragged her off to get dressed.

Ed and Swithbert, bringing clean clothes, shaving gear, and explanations for Christian, rushed in as the sisters rushed out.

IN WHAT SEEMED like no time, the wedding guests were reassembled on the terrace, which had been hastily put to rights by a platoon of servants. The audience couldn't be blamed for casting anxious glances over the parapet, considering what had appeared from that direction only a couple of hours earlier. But all they saw was the oncoming twilight, with its swathes of primrose and cinnabar, amethyst and ultramarine. None but Christian knew that this was Marigold's favorite time of day, with all her favorite colors.

Teddy, Harry, Willie, Ed, and the five dogs stood waiting beside the bishop on one side of the altar, and the triplets stood on the other side, as Swithbert and Marigold started down the aisle between the little gilt chairs. The princess was radiant in her pale pink linen (starting a fad in wedding gowns that lasted for decades), which was just the right match for Christian's crystal on a chain around her neck, the rubies in her best everyday tiara, and the cloud of plain, unadorned veiling that followed her down the aisle.

While everyone was watching the bride and her father approach, Christian stepped up to the altar, waiting with a look on his face that, if you didn't know how happy he was, might have been mistaken for mental impairment. So much had happened so fast, his mind was still trying to catch up and hadn't yet made it. The fact that he was standing next to his newly found brothers, who would also be his brothers-in-law, wasn't even the half of it.

Neither was the fact that he'd discovered his birthday was April 19, the same day as Marigold's. They were both fire signs, the most confident and dynamic combination.

The real half of it was that, in the deepest part of himself, he knew this was what he'd been headed toward for as long as he could remember. He'd been preparing for a life with Marigold—and for a life as a good king.

The wedding guests, when they turned in his direction, caught their breaths. *They* didn't think he looked mentally impaired. Not at all. Especially considering that the last time they'd seen him he'd been wearing dirty livery, hanging on to a rickety flying machine, and yelling at a couple of dogs to run faster. Now he was cleaned up, shaved, and splendid in fine leather breeches, an embroidered waistcoat, and a single diamond earring in his newly pierced ear. He wore a crown sparkling with gems—a borrowed crown, to be sure, but who except Christian and Swithbert had to know that?

But the guests were also looking as bewildered as Christian felt. Where was Magnus? Who *was* this new bridegroom? And where was Olympia?

Marigold and Christian stood before the bishop, hands clasped, eyes locked, knees weak, and heads reeling, repeating words they unequivocally meant with all their hearts.

Just before they were asked the question best answered by "I do," there came a commotion at the arched doorway. The guests could be excused for flinching and ducking reflexively. They had already had a great deal more commotion than most of them were used to.

"What's going on here? What are you doing be-hind my back?" Olympia came through the archway dressed in the most extravagant array—even for her—of silk, jewels, and furs that anyone had ever seen. "Stop the wedding!" she roared, rushing over with Fenleigh—freshly bathed and blown dry—clinging desperately to her shoulder. "*This* is the groom—" She dragged Magnus behind her. "Not *him*." She pointed at Christian. "We know nothing about him. He's an impostor, a . . . a *servant*." She spat the word.

There was total, stunned silence as she pulled Magnus down the aisle. He wouldn't look at anybody, just stumbled along after her, his head bowed.

Bub and Cate, as disoriented by the day's events as everyone else, went into fierce protective mode as they saw the ferocious queen bearing down on Ed and Chris. Bub ran at her, barking his head off, and Cate circled her, jumping and yipping and having a grand, dramatic time. The three floor mops, not wanting to be left out of the fun with their new friends, and having their own reasons for wanting to have a go at Olympia, joined in—crowding her, yapping and bump-ing, jumping for Fenleigh, creating new definitions of chaos.

The queen let go of Magnus, who hastily stepped back from the pandemonium. "Stop it!" Olympia said, flapping her hands at the animals and backing away. "Somebody get those monsters away from me!"

No one moved. Perhaps they were pausing to figure out just exactly how to enter the fray. Or what would most effectively lure the dogs away. Or how best to extricate the queen. Or maybe they were thinking that it was high time Olympia got what she deserved. Whatever their thoughts were would remain a mystery.

What happened was that Olympia backed against the terrace wall, the broken part that Christian, what with all that had been happening to him, had never finished repairing. And, with the dogs still after her, playing, or defending their loved ones, or just giving her a hard time—who can ever tell with dogs?—she tried to back up some more. The wall crumbled and gave way. Her feet went up, and she flipped backward over the side in a welter of gold lace, heavy brocade, thick furs, snapped necklaces that showered pearls across the terrace, and one frantic ferret.

By the time anyone from the stunned assemblage reached the wall to grab for her, it was too late. All that could be seen, in the fast-running river water, swollen with mountain snowmelt, was a puff of brocade skirt and a single silvery shoe with a curved heel and a bow on the toe. And even as they watched, those disappeared around a bend.

"Rollo!" the king ordered, in a voice of command that no one had heard from him in a very long time. "Go downriver and find her!" Rollo, with a sinking feeling that he already knew *how* they would find her, rushed off to assemble his troops.

In the same strong voice, Swithbert said, "Continue with the ceremony. We've had enough interrupted weddings around here for one day. We're going to get one finished."

Marigold and Christian were on their knees consoling the bewildered, whimpering dogs, who had the feeling that they'd done something seriously wrong but didn't know what.

Magnus, still standing where Olympia had left him, stammered, "B...b...but, what about m... m...me? I was supposed to be the bridegroom."

"Not anymore," Swithbert said. "Now sit down and keep quiet while we get Marigold and Chris hitched, and then you and I are going to have a chat. If things work out right, maybe we can find a spot for you to have your own little manor house."

Magnus shut his mouth and sat down so suddenly it looked as if his knees had been hit from behind.

Marigold and Christian finally got to say "I do." And when it came time to kiss the bride, Christian, who hadn't known what to do when Meg kissed him, somehow knew exactly what to do when the kissee was Marigold.

Then the guests rushed off to the Great Hall to carry on with the feasting that had been interrupted by the interrupted wedding.

Marigold and her sisters clustered around Swithbert. "Oh, Papa," they said, hugging him, "I'm sure Rollo will find Mother and bring her home."

"I'm not," Swithbert said, dry-eyed. "And if he does, I'll have to send her straight to the dungeon."

Well, the girls could hardly argue with him about that, but under the circumstances, they kept a tactful silence. Christian observed this and approved. It's exactly what the etiquette book would have advised: Refrain from bad-mouthing somebody when their situation looks particularly bleak.

He was happy to see that what he'd learned from Ed's book applied to royal life as well as to forest life, since he might soon actually need to know how to address a duke or recognize an oyster fork.

"You girls go down and mingle with the guests. I need to think. I'll join you later." So King Swithbert went off to his turret to think about what life might be like without Olympia, or maybe with an Olympia under better control than she'd been up to now. And what life would be like with Marigold gone off to Christian's kingdom.

"I'll go with you, Bert," Ed said. "I've got some thinking to do, too."

Swithbert wasn't used to people treating him like an ordinary person but decided he liked it, at least from Ed, so he said, "Come along, then." And off they went.

"Do you think it looks right to go to a party when our mother is—well, who knows where?" Eve, the most proper triplet, asked.

"To tell you the truth, I don't care how it looks," Marigold said. "This is my final wedding, and I'm going to enjoy it. When somebody is plotting to do you in, it's a little hard to feel sad when something bad happens to her." Her eyes filled for a moment, and she said softly, "I just wish I knew how she could even think of doing such a thing to her own daughter." Being one of the few royals practical enough to carry her own handkerchief, she wiped her eyes and turned to Christian. "Come along, my dearest heart," she said. "Let's go to our party." And they went off down the stairs, surrounded by dogs.

Eventually the other sisters joined them, and they all ended up having a very good time in spite of the need to remind themselves to look somber from time to time, since there was no word about Olympia.

By the time the festivities ended and everyone staggered off to bed, there was still no word.

At breakfast time Swithbert announced that all Rollo and his men had been able to find was the single shoe with the bow on the toe, so they were calling off the search. Wherever Olympia was, she would have to get along with only one shoe.

Just before dinner, when the last of the wedding guests had finally packed up and gone home, Swithbert called his family together in the library. He shut the doors and said, "Girls—and boys, too—I have some interesting news for you. Mrs. Clover came to me with a secret she's been keeping for years. One that she's kept until now only because Olympia threatened her with the iron maiden if she told. This will come as a shock to you girls, but I have to tell you that Olympia was not your real mother."

"*What?*" eight voices said in unison.

"That's right. She pretended to be expecting—she wanted to avoid the real thing because she thought it would be too hard on her figure—and she threatened Mrs. Clover into bringing babies to her in secret when the proper time came. Mrs. Clover says the babies were from decent village girls who had made mistakes and wanted good homes for their children. Mrs. Clover says she told the girls only that their babies would be going to noble families, so no one but Olympia and Mrs. Clover knew the whole truth."

"But then, who are we?" the triplets asked, holding each other's hands.

Swithbert scratched his head. "I don't know. The village Mrs. Clover brought you all from was burned to the ground and the inhabitants scattered during the last Visigoth raids, when you were little girls. So I guess you'll just have to be who you've always been."

"So you're not our papa?" Marigold asked, her lower lip trembling. Christian took her hand and stroked it.

King Swithbert took the other one. "*I* think I am," he said. "I'm the one who loved you all from the first moment I laid eyes on you, and who walked the floor with you when you were sick and played games with you and taught you to ride and shoot and cheat at cards. What else makes somebody a father?"

"You're right," Marigold said, and put the whole thing out of her mind, relieved to know that she was not related in any way to Olympia, who had done none of the things Swithbert had done for her. And further relieved to know why she had always felt as if she didn't quite fit into the life she had. Yet somehow, it seemed to fit better now that she knew all the parts of it. Secrets have a way of making themselves felt, even before you know there's a secret.

Christian spoke up. "Then Ed's my father. He did all those things for me. Except ride. We never had a horse." He knew he had another father over in Zandelphia, but that didn't mean Ed wasn't the real thing, too. And because he'd learned how sick King Beaufort was, Ed might soon be the only one.

"I'll teach you to ride," Marigold said.

"Will that make *you* my father?" Christian asked, teasing.

"So I APOLOGIZE to every one of you," Swithbert said humbly, "for marrying this person who was so bad for us all."

"But it was an arranged marriage, Papa," Marigold said. "You had no choice."

"I could have resisted harder, the way you did, Marigold, when all those suitors came calling. Or I could have controlled her more. I could have been a better king." He put his head in his hands. "I failed all of us, and my whole kingdom, terribly. I feel just awful."

"Start now," Ed said. "Be better now. If you could have done better before, you would have. But now that you have your act on the ball, you *can* do better. So start now." He was sounding parental, he knew it, but once a person had started with that job, it was a hard habit to break. Maybe breaking it was impossible. And didn't everybody need a little parenting from time to time, no matter how old or how royal they got? "All you have to do is keep your shoulder to the grindstone and your nose to the wheel."

Swithbert lifted his head. "Thank you, Ed. That's good advice. I think. I owe you one now."

"Okay," Ed said. "About Queen Mab..."

Epilogue

One Year Later

People eager for the ribbon cutting thronged the riverside terrace of Swithbert's castle. As they milled around, they could talk about nothing but the changes of the past year—so many that it was hard to believe it had been only a year since they had gathered here for Marigold's weddings to Magnus and then to Christian.

On this day every person in attendance was wearing one of Marigold's fragrances, now in full production by the ladies of both kingdoms of Zandelphia and Beaurivage. Once she'd been able to leave the castle and explore the forest, she had found many species of exotic flowers that made her scents much more complex and interesting. The demand for them was spreading throughout the known world—and adding revenues to both kingdoms' treasuries.

"Hello, Sir Magnus," Lady Buffleton said. "How are you? Your new manor house is about finished, I see."

"Yes, my lady," Magnus said. "I've been doing some of the work myself. I built a special room where I work on my maps—and some of them are pretty spectacular, if I do say so myself. I'm selling them to both Queen Mab and Tooth Troll Limited," he added proudly. "No one ever gets lost now." He handed her his card, designed with a little map of his estate. "I have p-mail, too," he said, pleased to be so modern.

All the local kingdoms were linked now by a p-mail system established by Christian—with the aid of Walter and Carrie and their offspring—who, now that he was King of Zandelphia, wanted easy communication with Swithbert, Ed, Tatiana and Willie, and a bunch of new friends, too.

"P-mail," Lady Buffleton mused, impressed by how relaxed and pleasant Sir Magnus was. Funny— she'd always thought of him as a nervous sort. Her unmarried daughter came to mind. Perhaps the two of them . . . She was interrupted from her matchmaking thoughts by King Swithbert strolling by and greeting her. "Oh, Your Majesty," she said to him, "I must say, the new decorations to the castle are simply—well, they're absolutely, well..."

"Oh, I know," Swithbert said. "Not everybody thinks baby teeth make good building material, but it *is* my castle, and I think they look splendid. We've been able to pave over almost all of the north turret with them since Ed opened up his Tooth Troll operation. Ed's eight brothers are helping him—nepotism is a troll tradition, you know. Same as royalty. And having Ed living here has really livened up the place. He's a fierce snipsnapsnorum player. I owe him a fortune, which is remarkable since we both cheat. Excuse me, I have to talk to Marigold."

Marigold and her sisters had been admiring Calista's and Eve's newest Norfolk terrier puppies from their best litter yet. They thought its success had something to do with their improved states of mind since they found out that they didn't have to be queens of Zandelphia. The puppies were four fat furry bundles on silver leashes. They had rolled and tumbled and played so much that their leashes were tangled, and the sisters were down on their knees trying to unsnarl them.

"Are you almost ready, Marigold?" Swithbert asked.

"As soon as I get this pup freed," she said. "Ah, there." She stood, dusting off her skirt. "Is Christian ready?"

"Waiting at the river." Swithbert signaled to the trumpeter, who blew a loud *ta-ra ta-ra* that silenced the throng.

"Time for the ceremony to begin," Swithbert said. He led the way down the stairs, through the castle, out the front gates (where Rollo was back on duty again, quite chastened after a few months in the dungeon for misusing his authority against Christian and Ed, and then receiving a medal for helping recover the lost heir of Zandelphia), across the drawbridge, and around the side of the castle to the river's edge. There Christian stood waiting, admiring his creation.

Marigold slipped her hand into the crook of his arm. "It's beautiful," she whispered into his ear, the one in which he wore his diamond earring. "I'm so proud of you."

"It *does* look good, doesn't it?" he said, putting his hand over hers. "And I can't think of anyone I'd rather have christen it."

Across the river hung a splendid new bridge, which Christian had designed and helped build. He called it a suspension bridge, and its arc was so clean and graceful, it made you stop and stare and think of things that weren't bridges at all, like eagles and courage and love.

As soon as all the people were assembled, Swithbert and Christian stood side by side and signaled for silence.

"Welcome to the Zandelphia-Beaurivage Bridge, linking our two kingdoms in friendship and commerce," Christian said. He didn't mention the ingenious devices that, in the event of an invasion, could make the bridge collapse, rendering it useless to enemies—and then restore it to its proper shape when the danger had passed. Survival depends upon acknowledging reality—and on keeping the necessary secrets.

Swithbert went on, "You're all invited to walk across the bridge to have a cool drink and sweetmeats at the cave-castle of King Christian and Queen Marigold of Zandelphia and then cross back over for feasting and entertainment at my castle in the beautiful, peaceful kingdom of Beaurivage. So, as soon as Marigold cuts the ribbon, let's go!"

Before an excited crowd (which included the blacksmith, who had been knighted for the outstanding deed of leaving the pieces of his failed flying machine stored in the dungeon, and Queen Mab, who was looking rather pushed out of shape, though quite a bit better rested), Christian handed Marigold the sharp dirk he kept in his boot, and she severed the purple ribbon across the end of the bridge as neat as you please. Then she linked arms with her father on one side and her husband on the other, and they started across.

"This time last year," Swithbert said, "if anybody had told me that I'd be a widower having the time of my life, and that my precious Marigold would be queen of the kingdom next door—"

"And that her castle would be a magical crystal cave that made her feel as if she were living inside the stars," Marigold added, "and that she'd be married to her best friend and the love of her life—"

"And that he'd be a *king*," Christian continued, "and someone whose inventions were in great demand, and that he'd be married to the queen of his heart, and be the happiest person in the world—"

"We'd have said that person was a lying lunatic!" they said in unison. Then they laughed all the way to the end of the bridge.

Once they reached Zandelphia, Christian and Marigold looked into each other's eyes. She said, "As long as we're with each other—"

"We know we're in exactly the right place," he finished.

The entrance to the cave had been fancied up, as befits a king's alternate residence, and a riverside terrace to match Swithbert's had been constructed next to the waterfall from which Christian had first seen Marigold. Of course, all Ed's collections had been moved into Swithbert's dungeons, so the cave didn't look quite as it had a year before. It was now more magnificent than ever, comfortably furnished and glittering extravagantly in the summer sunshine. The royalty taking tours of this alternate castle began to wish that they, too, had thought of living in a cave.

Marigold and Christian were already responsible for starting several other trends—such as watching the sunrise in their pj's (this one died out quickly as most royals didn't want to get up that early), eating vegetarian, wearing a single diamond earring, and using part of their residence as a home for unwanted children (this died out pretty fast, too, as most royals didn't really want to be bothered). Of course, for Christian and Marigold, these weren't trends at all— they were just the way the new king and queen of Zandelphia wanted to live their lives.

One trend Christian hoped would die out, at least with Marigold, were her awful jokes. Now that she could get out and about, she was hearing more of them, but they were all as bad as the ones she'd heard from the stable boy. Although he had to admit that he rather liked one: What side of a dragon has the most scales? Why, the outside, of course.

The sun shone in golden spears and birds sang cantatas as the guests drank lemonade and ate larks' tongue pâté and honey tarts. Marigold and Christian and Swithbert stood together with Calista and Teddy, Eve and Harry, Tatiana and Willie, and their frisky and adorable assorted children, watching the guests pack away the free refreshments. Slightly off to one side, Ed stood with Wendolyn, the red-haired troll maiden. Her father had had a sudden change of heart regarding Ed when he learned about Tooth Troll Limited, and the fact that it was operated out of King Swithbert's castle, not to mention that Ed now had an ODD Medal. They were each as happy as they could ever remember being in their entire lives.

They couldn't know that the next day would bring news of a woman who, one year ago, had been fished out of the river many miles downstream, half drowned, wearing one bow-toed silvery shoe, clutching a sopping ferret, and suffering from amnesia. It seemed that she had recently regained her memory.

CARPE DIEM EVER AFTER.